Francis Talbot O'Donoghue

St. Knighton's Keive: a Cornish tale

With a postscript and glossary

Francis Talbot O´Donoghue

St. Knighton's Keive: a Cornish tale
With a postscript and glossary

ISBN/EAN: 9783337174361

Printed in Europe, USA, Canada, Australia, Japan

Cover: Foto ©Andreas Hilbeck / pixelio.de

More available books at **www.hansebooks.com**

ST. KNIGHTON'S KEIVE:

ALE.

WITH A POSTSCRIPT AND GLOSSARY.

BY THE

REV. F. TALBOT O'DONOGHUE, B.A.,

VICAR OF TICKENHAM, SOMERSET, AND CHAPLAIN TO THE MARQUIS OF WESTMEATH.

"Their speech was not in Cornish phrase,
Their garb had marks of loftier days;
Slight food they took from hands of men,
They withered slowly in that glen.
One died!—the other's shrunken eye
Gush'd till the fount of tears was dry!
* * * *
They found her, silent, at the last,
But in the shape wherein she passed,
Where her lone seat long used to stand,
Her head upon her shrivell'd hand!"—HAWKER.

LONDON:

SMITH, ELDER AND CO., 65, CORNHILL.

M.DCCC.LXIV.

CONTENTS.

iv CONTENTS.

ST. KNIGHTON'S KEIVE,*

A CORNISH STORY.

CHAPTER I.

INTRODUCTORY.

"My instructions, Captain Will, are positive. There must be no intrusion upon the privacy of these ladies. So that if I take this cottage off your hands, I shall expect you to see that my orders are carried out to the very letter."

---

* Keeve, or Keive, means the basin or bowl, into which water falls from a cascade.

1

The speaker was a respectable middle-
aged solicitor, practising in the small country
town of Wadebridge, in the north of Cornwall, and the person he was addressing,
and who was perpetually shifting about in
his chair, and twirling his hat round and
round, was a little, cute-looking, bronze-
faced mine "captain," who, though still
in middle life, had been to almost all parts
of the world, wherever, that is, a mine was
to be worked, and who, like most of his
class, was full of intelligence, and keen and
sharp-sighted enough wherever his own
interests were at all concerned.

He was the owner, or rather he had
bought the lease, of a small house in the
cottage style, situated in St. Knighton's
Keive, which he had found great difficulty
in letting. Its situation was so remote, that
one look at it was usually quite enough
for any intending tenant, and the few who

had entered upon the occupancy of it had speedily thrown it up, alleging that the house was haunted, and the valley itself infested with goblins. Hence, no one could be induced to remain in the house for more than a week or two, and Captain Will (who, by the way, had a mortal dread of the place himself, and was a firm believer in all the ghost stories told of it), had the mortification, time after time, of having the key of the house returned to him, with a message, perhaps, that nothing would induce the person who brought it to sleep another night in the house. The cottage was too good a one to be pulled down, having been built with a view to the accommodation of the person who rented the mill—the only other building in the valley. But somehow the man could never be induced to reside in it, and preferred walking some distance every morning to

his work from the little fishing village of
Mawnan Porth, about two miles distant
from the valley, and returning in the evening. Altogether Captain Will's speculation
had not turned out very well up to this
time. What was his delight, then, to receive
a message one morning from the "great
office" (as it used to be called), in Wadebridge, desiring him to call there, as Mr.
Pearce wished to speak to him about his
house in St. Knighton's Keive.

Captain Will was a great deal too cute
to give any tokens of his real feelings.
Though amazed at heart how anybody could
think of living in such a place, if he could
by possibility contrive to live elsewhere,
yet he thought it well in his interview with
the lawyer to dilate not a little upon the
romantic beauty of the spot, upon its quietness, upon the village being so handy to
it, upon the fine coast almost within sight.

He even dropped some hints of going to live there himself, his "missus" had taken such a "mighty fancy" to the place. Mr. Pearce understood his man a great deal too well to attach any sort of importance to what he said in praise of St. Knighton's Cottage, as it was called, and knew that this bold Cornish captain would as soon think of facing a legion of devils as be found in the bewitched valley after dark. Accordingly, after a good deal of haggling, a bargain was struck between them, and the rent agreed upon.

"I will be answerable for the rent," said Mr. Pearce to him, "and all communications respecting the place must be made to me alone, and in no instance whatever to the ladies themselves who are coming to occupy it. You will please understand, Captain Will," went on Mr. Pearce, "that neither you, nor anybody by your authority, or with your connivance, is to approach the house during its occupancy by these ladies. Whatever you have got to say about it, must be said to me."

" Deuce a fear of my going near the place," said Captain Will, who no longer thought it necessary to keep up any appearance of being desirous to inhabit the house himself. " I always require to take a sup of drink more than usual " (for the captain was a thirsty soul) " after being there."

" Well, now, Captain Will, there are two or three things we have got to arrange about. I know nothing myself of these ladies who are coming. I don't even know their names. My instructions are entirely from Messrs. Wenlock and Gooch, the great London solicitors, and they have merely written to make inquiries on behalf of a client of theirs—a person of rank, they say, but whom they don't reveal—to ascertain if there is any very retired dwelling to be rented somewhere in the north of Cornwall —it doesn't much matter where, so that it be remote from other dwelling-houses; the more remote, they say, the better."

" Egad, my house is just the place for them, then."

" They leave all the necessary arrangements to me, about furnishing the house, and making everything fit for the reception of these two ladies. So that, Captain Will, I think I had better go over with you to St. Knighton to-morrow, and, if I like the furniture, which you say is in the house already, and we can come to terms about it, I have no objection to purchase everything just as it stands. For the house is wanted immediately; and if there is anything more required we can put it in without delay. And there is another thing, Captain Will; we must make out this man of the mill, and arrange with him to supply these ladies with everything they want. They are to write out, I believe, a list of what they require, and leave it for him in some fixed place; but, as I understand, no one is to have any personal communication with them on any pretence whatever — neither parson, nor doctor, nor anybody else—except by my orders."

" Why, sir," said Captain Will, getting up and preparing to leave the room, " it will give the valley a worse name than ever, to have two such ladies living at the cottage. To speak to nobody! not even to Tom Bawden of the mill! Well, it is a rum go!"

" I am paying you a good rent, and you are in luck to have found a tenant at last," said Mr. Pearce. " I will call for you, then, to-morrow, and drive you out in my gig."

"We must go early, sir, if we want to catch Bawden. He never stops at the mill longer than he can help. It is so lonesome like, he says."

"Well, this is early in the summer, and it is not likely he will be gone before five or six. We shall have a good deal to do at the house."

"Better start early, sir," persisted Captain Will, "so that we can get away in good time. If you have never seen the place, as you say you haven't, it is about the dismallest place you ever put foot in."

"Though you said it was so lovely just now. Ah! Captain Will! Captain Will!"

"All fair, sir, in the way of business. Why should I go crying down my property?" And with these words Captain Will took his departure, hugely delighted at the stroke of business he had done that morning.

Let us accompany Mr. Pearce and the
mine captain in their excursion next day to
St. Knighton's Keive.

The north coast of Cornwall, as is well
known, abounds in beautiful sequestered
valleys. Side by side with the barest,
bleakest scenery, you come every now and
then upon valleys of exquisite beauty. You
have, perhaps, scarcely seen a tree or a
shrub for miles, but all at once you descend
into some shady ravine, thick with oaks and
ash trees, stunted, indeed, in size, and bent
from the effects of many a gale. Of these
valleys, St. Knighton's is at once the most
sequestered and richest in foliage of all
sorts. It is a miniature forest. Trees, fern,
brambles, all growing together. It is so
now, and so it was thirty and forty years
ago—as long as anybody can recollect. No
axe is ever heard ringing through its precincts, and, save for the water falling from a

cascade thirty feet in height, and the occasional noise of the mill, an unbroken silence
prevails. There are sloping hills on each
side, and a huge barrier of rock at the head
of the valley. Trees rising above trees at
the sides, and the thickness of the bushes,
effectually shut out the sun's rays, and on
the brightest morning an awful twilight
seems to prevail. There it is " always
afternoon." Upon a small cleared space of
ground, just near the waterfall and the
barrier of rocks referred to, may still be seen
the ruinous walls of what was once a cottage
of some size. These walls are now covered
with ivy, and overgrown with fern and wild
clematis. There are a few slight remains of
windows and doors, and here and there
portions of the old stone floors. It is now
the picture of desolation. Travellers speak
of it as the home of toads and noisome
reptiles. Yet was it once the shelter of

youth and beauty. Those walls, now covered over with lichen and moss, and where the ivy spreads itself at will, once echoed to the cry of the forsaken and stricken one—have witnessed the pangs of hopeless sorrow, the keen sharp struggle with despair, the last great struggle of all !

To Mr. Pearce's eyes, when he visited it, along with his companion from Wadebridge, it presented all the appearance of a neat compact cottage, with some half dozen small rooms in it, besides the kitchen and out offices. In front was a small flower garden, and behind the house upon a slope of the hill was laid out a tolerably sized kitchen garden. The silence, save for the splashing of the waterfall hard by, and the occasional twittering of a bird, was complete. And Mr. Pearce could hardly wonder at his companion's visible reluctance to stay in such a place any longer than was absolutely necessary. " Sure, sir," he would say every now and then, "we can go on to the 'Wortley Arms,' or to the 'Castle Inn,' at Mawnan, and finish our business there. This place gives one the horrors, and all that, it does."

The business that brought them was at length despatched to the captain's no small contentment. A list of the things required was made out, and an arrangement entered into with the man of the mill, who had been fetched up by Captain Will, as to supplying the inmates of the cottage with all they required, and in such a way as not to intrude upon that privacy which was so much insisted on in all the instructions received from town, and which, it was said, was intended to be absolute and unbroken. On a certain day the house was to be prepared by the miller's wife for the reception of two of the ladies. No servant was to be kept, only a char-woman for a few hours every day. Nor was any one to be in waiting to receive them. Having given these instructions, Mr. Pearce and Captain Will returned to Wadebridge.

CHAPTER II.

REGINALD TRELAWNEY.

"I AM afraid I have something of the vagrant about me—I often think I should like to live amongst my native hills,— Cheshire is too flat and tame for me;" this was what the Rev. Reginald Trelawney said to his patron, Sir Philip Cholmondeley, as they were sitting together late one evening smoking their pipes in the baronet's library at Cholmondeley Hall in Cheshire. Sir Philip, who had taken up with very High Church notions, had built a beautiful chapel—quite a gem in its way—adjoining

his house, and here a daily choral service
was celebrated. He appeared to have been
fortunate in his selection of a chaplain—
as far at least as this went,—that each
seemed exactly to suit the other. Both
were very musical, and this circumstance
alone formed, as it usually does, a bond of
union between them. And then Mr. Trelawney was a single man—sure to be of
good family from his name, though little
was known of his antecedents. Then he
was tall, handsome, and good-looking—say
about eight and twenty—very dark com-
plexioned, with fine eyes, and hair coal-
black. He might have been taken for a
Spaniard, he was so dark and grave. To
a proud reserved man, like Sir Philip Cholmondeley, Mr. Trelawney was very accept-
able. He was well informed, had travelled
a good deal, could describe well what he
had seen, and had the easy, well-bred polish

of a man of the world. Again, he very seldom ever spoke of himself, or alluded to his previous history. He had not been long in orders, and had never been known to assign any reason for entering the ministry at so comparatively late a period; so that there was no danger of his offending. his patron by any undue propensity to talk about himself, or his belongings. He had not apparently much of a theological turn, and never by any accident attended "clerical meetings," or seemed to care to cultivate the acquaintance of his clerical neighbours. Thus, little was known of him by his brother clergy, and they could only vaguely guess at his opinions. All was mere surmise. He was no controversialist, that was certain, and seemed rather to despise polemical disputes than care to understand them, or take any part in them. He was then an inscrutable problem to most who came in contact with him, but not to his patron, who liked him well enough, and thonght he understood him. People in general were rather afraid of him, and set him down as " satirical," from not knowing what else exactly to say about him. There was an air of preoccupation about him, as if his thoughts were far away, and not always very agreeably engaged, which is never viewed with much favour in society, and which induced most people to set him down as a dreamy; absent, inscrutable sort of man, of whom little could be made. Even the young ladies could make nothing of him, much as they might admire his dark eyes, or feel interested in the air of melancholy which was the ordinary expression of his countenance. And so now upon this June night, and sitting over the fire in Sir Philip's library, smoking their pipes, Trelawney gave utterance to that restless feeling, and desire of change, which Sir Philip had latterly noticed in him, having often indeed heard him say much the same thing on former occasions.

"You see, Sir Philip, I have Cornish blood in my veins, and feel often a restless longing for the land of my fathers,—for the granity hills of Cornwall, bare and bleak though they look, and to hear the roar of the ocean once more dashing up against the cliffs."

"You have not been in Cornwall lately, have you, Trelawney?"

"No, not for several years, but there are some things one can never get out of one's head; and the wide extensive moors covered with heath, and those bare hills strewn over with gigantic masses of rock, possess an interest for me, which I suppose none but a Cornishman, bred and born, can comprehend."

"Well, I can't pretend to share your admiration from my recollection of the county, when I travelled through it the year before last. I came by coach from Exeter, and a more dreary, desolate country than that which lies between Exeter and Truro can hardly be imagined."

"It is the least picturesque of the routes, no doubt."

"Picturesque, my dear fellow; what can you be thinking about? Why, it was the abomination of desolation itself, as far as I could see."

"And yet you will admit that, even travelling by that route, unpromising as it looked, you passed the two highest hills in the West of England—Rowter, and Brown Willy; you skirted Dartmoor, and were frequently during the day within a short walk of some of the finest coast scenery in all England; you were near some of

the most beautiful valleys that the foot of
man ever trod—the Vale of Lanherne,
for instance, with its ancient convent of
Carmelite nuns."

"Well, I don't remember anything of
that sort—I speak merely from a general
impression."

Trelawney's eye kindled, and his voice
betrayed an unusual emotion for him while
speaking. After this, they smoked on in
silence for a considerable while. At length
Trelawney reverted to his first subject.

"I have a sort of notion, Sir Philip,
that downright, good hard work would be
the best thing in the world for me. It is
all very pleasant this sort of life I lead
here with you—almost under your roof, and
as if I was a member of your family;
and the time was, when I dreamt that a
perpetual round of holy services, day after
day, and these glorious chants which we

sing in your chapel, and the ample oppor-
tunities afforded me for study and reading
in your library—that these all would have
brought peace with them—that I should
have found happiness in such quiet pursuits. But, Sir Philip, I have not. I am
not able to enter into explanations. It is
only that I feel the need of exertion—of
leading an active life—if I am ever to be
happy or at peace again, and I feel strongly
inclined to undertake the charge of that
large mining parish in the west of Cornwall, which I told you a college friend of
mine had offered me."

"Hadn't you better talk to my brother
Henry and his wife? You know them
both very well, and they may be able to
give you advice which may help you. A
brother clergyman might be able to enter
into your feelings, better than a dull
country squire like myself. Do, Trelawney,"

said Sir Philip, kindly, as he could not be blind to the unusual emotion displayed by his friend. "Speak to Henry, and if he can induce you to alter your mind and stop, you know how delighted I shall be, and so will Lady Cholmondeley, for that matter."

"I am afraid it is of no use. I am sure I feel your kindness very sensibly, Sir Philip, but I have at times such an irresistible longing for Cornwall,—I suppose it is the Cornish blood stirring in my veins. What else it is, God knows! My rest is so broken now, and I have such strange dreams, and all running upon the same thing. Last night I had a dreadful one. I dreamt that I was in some dark gloomy valley. I heard the waves of the sea dashing up against the cliffs. It seemed evening. There were a great many trees, and they were completely arched over head. There was fern

and lonely dank grass growing all about.
I remember standing by the side of a running stream. There was a waterfall and
a mill a little way off, which seemed to be
shut up. All around seemed so lonely and
deserted,—when of a sudden a female figure
started up by my side, and her face—oh,
what a sad one it was! It was so pale
and wasted, and she looked at me with
those fixed, stony, grey eyes of hers, but
said nothing. Only her lips moved, and
she wrung her hands and pointed towards
the waterfall. And then I saw a tall figure
in black, closely veiled, coming towards us,
and she lifted her veil, and oh, my God!
who did I see?—one, Sir Philip, who has
been dearer to me than my own soul—one
of whom I have been cruelly robbed—one
whose fate has been hitherto wrapped up
in mystery. Oh, my God! can she be in
such a dreadful lonely place as I beheld in

my dream — alone with such a companion ? ''

Trelawney's emotion seemed to shake his
frame. He was usually so impassive. But
now the pent-up sorrow of years burst forth
in an agony of grief, and his friend—who
had never imagined that a man whom the
world reputed so cynical and heartless,
could be thus overcome—sought in vain for
some minutes to afford him consolation.

"I am a fool," at length he said, "to
be thus overcome, and I ought not to have
inflicted such a gloomy tale upon you, Sir
Philip, and at such an unconscionable hour
—for it is nearly twelve o'clock. However,
I awoke much disturbed this morning, and
all day long the dream has haunted me."

"Well, dreams do play us odd tricks at
times," said Sir Philip, pushing back his
chair, and making preparations to retire.

"Yes; and what is more extraordinary,"

went on Trelawney, partly musing with himself, "I have had the same dream, or something very like it, before. Only one time I seemed to myself to be walking on the sea-shore,—some wild desolate shore,—and the tide was coming in fast, and dashing up against the rocks, and threatening to sweep me away, and I endeavoured to climb up the face of some enormous high cliff, and when I got half-way I missed my footing, and tried to catch at something, but fell—fell from such a height, and the fright awoke me. Well, good-night, Sir Philip, I must think the matter over, and at any rate will do nothing in a hurry."

CHAPTER III.

ST. MAWNAN PORTH.

THE reader must please to fancy himself, or herself, in a small remote fishing village on the north coast of Cornwall. It consists of two or three very narrow streets. The houses are small and shabby, and the smell of fish and sea-weed pervade them extensively. The men are lounging about in all directions—tawny, dark visaged, resolute looking fellows—some few with rings in their ears. Most of them have been out in their boats the night before, and their wives and daughters have gone to sell the fish that was caught; or a cart, perhaps, has taken some of it into Camel-ford and the neighbourhood. There is a glorious sea stretching out before you. The water is of the deepest blue,—where is there such marine blue as in Cornwall? —and right and left, as you cast your eye along the coast, are to be seen huge masses of rock, some towering in the air, some running out far into the sea. Here, there is a rock standing up alone at a little distance from the shore, and the top of which is covered with gulls; and, if you are very fortunate indeed, you may perchance see a little further up the coast that now rare bird the Cornish chough, with his raven black plumage and bright red beak and legs. A few boats are out, their sails lazily flapping to the slight June breeze. Here there is a gentle murmur, as the wave breaks softly on the white sand at your feet, while far away

in the distance to the right may be heard a
dull booming sound, as the sea is borne in
upon the

" Thundering shores of Bude and Boss."

The houses of this little village are
quaint, old-fashioned dwellings, mostly con-
structed of stone, rude and unshapely, much
as they were hewed from the rock.   A dash
of whitewash relieves their prevalent colour,
and promotes the salubrity of the little fishing community.   The parish church is two
or three miles off; so a little whitewashed
meeting-house, with staring windows dispro-
portionately large, does duty instead; and
from its unpainted deal pulpit spiritually-
minded cobblers, and precocious youths, and
even women with a " gift" (for the chapel
belongs to the Bible Christians, and has a
great B. C., with the year of the Lord carved
in stone over its principal entrance), have an

opportunity every Sunday, and on one week-day evening, of edifying the primitive dwellers at Mawnan Porth.

Upon this particular morning there is a little knot of fishermen conversing together, just where they have spread their nets to dry over the iron rails that protect the side of the road next the sea, and where they can descry every object within the range of vision.

Some of them are smoking, some of them sitting on the low wall splicing ropes, and one weather-beaten old tar, with a great deal of white beard, and with yellow wrinkled face, and who might have been the "Ancient Mariner" himself, with those bright glitter-ing eyes of his, was occasionally sweeping the horizon with a well-worn telescope.

" Come, tell us all about it, Tom," said one of them to his fellow, a middle-aged looking man, with blue Jersey, and hand-kerchief tied loosely about his neck.

" Why, you see, our Rosina," was the reply, " thought that she might as well take some fish which she hadn't sold down to the cottage at St. Knighton's, as she heard tell that there were somebody living there now. But she had hardly set foot in the valley before she was stopped by Tom Bawden of the mill, who said that no one must on no account go next or nigh the cottage, for, says he, ' there be ladies there now who must not be spoken to, or gone nigh to at all.' ' That be a queer fashion to live in,' said our little maid, just that way. ' Well, that is neither here nor there,' answered Tom, roughly ; ' my orders be positive, forby one of the ladies it is my belief and opinion,' says he, ' cannot utter a word—is deaf and dumb like.' ' What makes you think that?' asked Rosy. ' Why,' says Tom, ' I am bidden to go up to the cottage every Monday morning for orders, which are left in a little

box that has been made in the gate on
purpose like, and then next day,' says he, ' I
mostly brings the things from Carnelford
that were ordered; and I have to leave them
in a little outhouse which is not used for
anything. And so,' says Tom, ' on the first
Tuesday that I was up there to leave the
things, I met one of the ladies just as I was
returning; and so says I to her, taking off my
hat to her at the same time quite civil, ' I
have left the things, ma'am, where I was
bid.' 'And what did she say to that?' asked
our little maid. ' Oh, she just put her
hand to her lips, and made a sign as if she
couldn't speak, or wouldn't, at any rate.'
Then Rosina asked Tom what she was like,
and he made answer that she was a lady, not
old at all, but very sad and melancholy like.
She seemed, however, to thank Tom, for
she bowed her head, and returned to the
house."

" Well, that's queer enough," was the comment of one of the listening fishermen, as he proceeded to put some more tobacco in his pipe.

" And I am told," says another, " and that by one that was about when they arrived, that they were driven to the house in a hired carriage, which seemed to have come from some distance, and that there was only one man with them, who looked like a servant, only he wasn't in livery, and that he stayed but a short time—just long enough to help to bring the boxes and other things into the house, and then drove off in the carriage he had come in—only this time he got inside it."

" It is said," put in another, " that they walk out most days, but have never quitted the valley. They be collecting ferns and wild-flowers."

" And some do say snails and slugs: for

to eat, I suppose," added a young sailor,
who had not before spoken.

"One of them be uncommon pretty, I
hear; but it is hard to catch a glimpse of
them, as they have mostly their veils over
their faces. They be nearly a height, and
from what I hear, there is not much difference in their ages."

While this conversation was proceeding,
if any of the party had taken a walk about
a mile inland, in the direction of St.
Knighton's Keive, he might have had an
opportunity of forming his own judgment
respecting these mysterious strangers whose
arrival had afforded a subject of gossip in
every farmhouse and cottage about the
neighbourhood. For, walking up and down
not far from their cottage, one of them
occasionally stopping to gather a fern, or
piece of heath, or a wild flower, were two
ladies, both dressed very simply in black.

No conversation passed between them, but, as there was an occasional interchange of signs, it might be presumed that one or other of them—she, probably, who looked a trifle the oldest, say about eight-and-twenty, and whose pale, sad face wore that fixed, stony appearance—was afflicted with that great calamity, the loss of speech and hearing. To a close observer, a disparity of rank between the parties might have been inferred. The taller and younger of the two walked a trifle in advance of her companion, and was never addressed first by her. Occasionally, by a rapid motion of the fingers, she would seem to make a remark or ask a question of her companion, and the answer to it would be briefly communicated in the same manner. The younger lady's dress, too, was of somewhat richer material than her companion's, and she wore several rings of value upon her long delicate, tapering fingers, which the other did not. Altogether the relationship between them was probably that of a lady and her companion or attendant. And now that the younger lady has lifted up that thick veil which had partly concealed her features, the difference of rank between them was more conspicuous. Her age might be about five or six and twenty. She had that clear, olive complexion, with brown eyes, and profusion of dark hair which would have attracted admiration seen anywhere. Added to which that, though participating to some extent in the air of sadness which was the prevailing expression of her companion's face, yet the effect was rather to chasten than altogether to obscure that cheerfulness of mien which seemed to be natural to her. Even the discovery of some little wild flower in its shady recess, or the acquisition of a rare fern, lighted up those lovely features with a transient glow of pleasure, and made her eyes to sparkle. There was a lightness and elasticity, too, in her carriage, which contrasted with the more sedate movements of her companion.

After a time the ladies might have been seen slowly retracing their steps towards the cottage, where we must leave them for the present.

CHAPTER IV.

A CORNISH MINE.

MONTACUTE is the name of a new ecclesi-
astical district carved out of the old parish
of St. Swithun in West Cornwall. The
population is mostly mining, but there is
a tolerable sprinkling of farmers and agri-
cultural labourers as well. Still everybody
there has something to do with the mines.
These enter largely into every one's calcu-
lation who adopts a profession, or sets up in
business in those parts. Is a man going to
be a doctor,—to purchase a practice there?
The great question to be determined is,
what mines can he secure? to what mines

can he obtain the appointment of surgeon? Or, if a lawyer, then there are purserships going, snug comfortable things in their way. Or it may be that a mine which has been "knacked," or which is "shaky," requires to be set going again. Who so fit for this as a lawyer? Say Lawyer Gully from the neighbouring town of Penpoll; who can compare to him in fertility of schemes? Suppose ten thousand pounds is wanted. The thing is easily done. Issue a couple of thousand shares at a pound a-piece, and they will be soon taken up in the neighbourhood. Never fear, if Lawyer Gully once sets his mind upon it. One man buys a lot in order to dispose of them the very first moment he can turn a penny by them. Only run up the shares somehow — the purser knows how to manage *that*—and see what a handsome profit is realized by this early speculator! Another takes shares because Lawyer

Gully has made him a promise that he shall supply the mine with wine and spirits. And what a good thing is to be made out of that with a little cleverness! Or, it is the Foundry company in the neighbouring town of Tregurgle, or the well-to-do draper in Penpoll; —every one hopes to serve his own purpose by helping to set the mine going. What an advantage it will be to Penpoll, where trade is so stagnant, to have such a mine as Wheal Ann at work again! Think of all the wages that will be spent there! What a roaring business the inns and public houses will do! For was there ever a mine captain yet who didn't love his glass, and two glasses better than one? Publicans, butchers, and all, must take shares, just to set the thing a-going, afterwards they can do what they like with them, so Lawyer Gully tells them with a wink out of those keen grey eyes of his. He is a great man in Penpoll is Lawyer Gully, and lives in that large handsome house with its beautifully laid-out grounds on the right, just as you enter the town. How he came by them, it boots not to say. The story is an old one now, and the last person more particularly interested in it died in a lunatic asylum, or workhouse, or some such place, where the weak get shoved into to die. However, this troubles not Lawyer Gully, as he bustles about disposing of no end of shares. He is looked upon as the great benefactor of Penpoll, and is spoken of already as the next mayor, the future M.P., Heaven knows what! Now, see he has taken aside that needy little Cornish baronet; see how he describes to him what great things Wheal Ann is going to do; what fortunes are to be made out of her. He whispers something in his ear about London adventurers, and Captain Dick, and a certain piece of

copper ore which the captain has been dis-
playing to some purpose, as it would seem,
in town, and which he swears has come
from Wheal Ann. What is it, then? The
little Cornish baronet is "lord of the set"
about to be worked. The dues are to
enrich him beyond his wildest hopes, so
he must put down his name for fifty shares
at least. The little baronet makes some
demur about it. He is not so easily talked
over as all that. Besides, he knows his
man, and how that fine house and grounds
of his have been come by, quite eclipsing
as they do his own hereditary and dilapi-
dated mansion of Treherne; and he knows
who pays for all the champagne and claret
that flow so freely at the lawyer's hospitable table, quite shaming his own "dinner
sherry" and thirty-two shilling port, and
he has heard more queer stories about
Lawyer Gully than he quite relishes.

However, he is in the strong man's grasp, both literally and metaphorically. Gully would be a dangerous man to make an enemy of. Was he ever known to stop at anything? And then, How about that mortgage money on Treherne? Might he not play him an ugly trick and call in the money? So down goes Sir Roger Pendragon's name for the fifty shares, and the lawyer walks off well pleased with his success, for all the shares intended for the neighbourhood are now disposed of. It is a slightly curious circumstance about the affair that, eager as the lawyer has been about disposing of the shares, yet he has taken none himself. He spoke, indeed, at the mine dinner, in that capital speech of his, which he delivered after the cloth had been removed, grace said, and the Queen's health drank, of the fifty shares he would at once put his own name down for. But perhaps he did not bespeak them in time, or something of that sort; for certain it is that no shares were ever assigned to him; or was it that he was aware that every shareholder, as a partner, makes himself answerable for all the debts of the mine? Poor Sir Roger, as if you had not debts enough of your own without being saddled with the debts of the mine!

No difficulty is anticipated in London by this expert man of business. Captain Dick has prepared the way for him with his "specimens," which he is ready to swear came direct from Wheal Ann, and there were plenty of gudgeons swimming all round, and drinking in everything the "Captain" let fall—all eagerness to make their fortunes in the Cornish mines, a feat represented by Captain Dick to be something easier than picking blackberries off the hedges in October. Then arrives upon the scene Lawyer Gully from Penpoll, full of the *furor* to obtain shares which he alleges to exist in his own neighbourhood. The list of names is produced, headed by that of Sir Roger Pendragon. It could be easily doubled or trebled if thought desirable. But "London friends" must not be forgotten ; and so the remaining 8,000*l.* worth of shares is soon got rid of.

With this closes Lawyer Gully's share of the business. He pockets his cool five hundred pounds clear of travelling and hotel expenses—nearly a tenth more—and washes his hands of the mine. Shares are tendered to him at par—he declines them with thanks. The pursership is pressed upon him ; he shakes his head in a jocular manner, and will have none of it.

The mine now enters upon phase number two. It is soon understood that the

shares are almost entirely in the hands
of London "adventurers." Somehow or
other, the Foundry company, the wine
merchant, the prosperous draper in Penpoll; they have all quietly slipped out of
the business—disposed of their shares in
the London market at a small premium.
They can now afford to take matters quietly,
—get all the gain they can arising from
labourers' wages and expenditure at the
mine, and leave the risk, and probably
eventual loss, to strangers in London and
elsewhere. But there is little sign, indeed,
of failure at the first going off. Was
there ever such a powerful engine con-
structed before—of I don't know how
many horse power. Why, the cylinder of it
is so large that the directors and Lawyer
Gully are going to have a dinner in it,
and then a sketch of it is to appear in
the *Illustrated London News.*

It was a bright idea with whomsoever it originated, for it sent up the shares immediately. And then what wonderful things are to be done in the way of schools for the miners' children, sick clubs, and the like! Nothing sectarian, however, about them! The clergyman is to have nothing to do with them. This was an express stipulation. The directors are a motly group. There is a Jew among them, two or three atheists, a Socinian, and a "liberal-minded" Churchman, who thinks all sects much alike, and then there is the fashionable secretary, or manager, who sports a moustache and large whiskers, and comes out strong in chains and rings. He would be handsome, but for that flushed face of his, attributable, it may be (as he says) to over work, or possibly to that open bottle of sherry which is perpetually at his elbow, and which he imparts liberally, it must be

admitted, to all comers of the right stamp
—that is, persons who are worth the com-
pliment. This secretary is a tremendous
fellow at "Rules for the workmen." He
allows no one to swear on the mine, except
himself, of course, and any Director who
may have a turn that way. He is not
religious, he says, but his wife is, (she
is *really* a good kind of woman, but
conscientiously blind to her husband's failings), and so the Sabbath is to be kept
holy on the mine, and the workmen en-
joined to attend a place of worship. It
was time now that Wheal Ann should be
making some return to the adventurers,
for heavy and numerous had been the
"calls." There was no denying that everything was of the best sort—engines, pumps,
ladders, &c. The horse and trap in which
the secretary drove about was quite a credit
to the mine, so were the dinners, the wine,

and the spirits, all first-rate — dear, certainly, but good of the kind, which was a great matter, as the secretary used to observe. At last the ten thousand pounds was got through; ugly whispers were abroad —there was an execution at the mine, put in by the Foundry Company. No account of the secretary. In a week all was still, and as silent at Wheal Ann as ever. The loss fell exclusively upon "foreigners," (as inhabitants out of the Duchy are styled), and this was the only thing the adventurers ever had to divide amongst them.

Wheal Ann had been one of the principal mines in St. Swithun, and when Mr. Trelawney was appointed, as he was through the interest of the vicar, to the incumbency of the district church, the halcyon days of the mine had just come to an end as related above.

CHAPTER V.

MONTACUTE.

MR. TRELAWNEY, though a native of Cornwall, had not visited the county for several years, and found himself almost a stranger there when he arrived at Montacute. He had ·no very near relations living in Cornwall, and, with the exception of the vicar of St. Swithun, Mr. Praed, who resided upon another living at a distance, had no acquaintances amongst the clergy. St. Swithun, of which, as we have said, Montacute formed a part, is an extensive mining parish. The natural features of the country are, however, interesting.

The Montacute chain of hills, from which one of the finest views in the county is to be had, runs in a direction east and west. Bare and bleak-looking are these hills at first sight. But, as you ascend them, patches of purple heath meet the eye, and golden furze, and gorse, and fern. Wild enough is it surely as you approach the cone-shaped summit, with its immense boulders, and huge masses of rock, scattered in all directions. And then, when at the very top, seated on that large splinter of rock which seems to have been thrown off by some convulsion of nature, what a view presents itself. Trelawney was enchanted with it on the first morning he ascended the hill. A soft balmy gentle morning in July it was, with the breeze just stirring, wafting the scent of the furze blossom, and seeming fraught with memories of the past, with tender soothing memories of the living and the dead, of the absent and estranged. There in the distance, on two sides of you, lay the sea gleaming like molten silver, calm and motionless, under the influence of the summer's sun; little specks of sails, or the smoke of a steamer being just perceptible, and rising proudly out of the sea St. Michael's Mount,—that object which (with the exception of the Land's End) we associate more than any other with Cornwall.

"Ah," thought Trelawney as he gazed on it with interest for the first time, "how many stirring events in English history has not that Mount been the scene of—to have been resorted to for trade by the Phœnicians when the Greeks were besieging Troy, and the Jews building their Temple,—to have been a monastery, and object of pilgrimage, like its namesake in Normandy, during the middle ages, to Wes-

tern Christendom,—to have been seized
on by Perkin Warbeck, to have received
Charles I., and held out for the royal cause
during the civil wars—how many associations
does not that towering mass of rock bring
to the mind!" Or did Trelawney's eye rest
on the little valleys here and there, or on
those clumps of trees scattered up and
down, and encircling some homestead, or on
the massive granite church towers studded
about the bay, or on yon tapering spire
more inland rising out from amongst the
trees in the distance,—all on that soft hazy
July morning spoke of peace and repose.
Elevated as he was five hundred feet above
the level of the sea, even the clanking sound
of the "stamps" did not seem out of place,
giving just enough of life to the scene to
prevent it from oppressing the spirits. All
around and above breathed of peace then
on that calm lovely July morning, with its

perfumed air, and the elastic heathery turf
at your feet.

But had Trelawney found the peace he
sought? Had he left all his cares behind
him in the far north-west as he had fondly
hoped? Alas! no. The storm raged in
his breast at times more fiercely than ever.
And then the sense of loneliness and desolation, and uprooting of habits which had
become second nature, quite oppressed him
with melancholy. "Why seek her out?"
he thought. "She is another's. And if
I were to discover where that bad, cruel
man has had her conveyed, what but misery
—what but ruin and misery could befall us
both? Better—better we never meet again.
I have gone through the worst; I have
drank the cup of bitterness to the very
dregs; why revive it all?" Thus did
Trelawney's thoughts battle with each other
as he gazed down on that fair quiet scene

all around; on that tapering spire pointed
up to heaven; on those peaceful homesteads
in different directions, each looking a picture
of repose and of quiet home happiness.
" Ah," he thought, " what has led me here?
Is it mere fancy that has disturbed all my
thoughts, distorted my dreams? Is there
anything in what I have dreamt—in that
mysterious hand beckoning to me? Is it for
good or evil I have come here?" "What
dost thou here, Elijah?" The words rose
to his lips, as conscious of a fierce inex-
tinguishable fire raging in his bosom; of
a longing, unappeasable desire to look upon
that face once more that had wrought him
so much misery, and to touch that hand
yet once again—that plighted, betrothed
hand, which had been so cruelly wrested
from him. With these conflicting thoughts,
which one while would lead him to seek
safety in flight—to put whole oceans be-

tween him and the ill-fated object of his
passion; and, in a moment afterwards, to
hug his secret to his bosom—to revel and
delight in the chance of discovering his
long lost one; of rescuing her from misery;
of drying her tears; of bursting open the
doors of her prison-house, and bearing her
off triumphant to far distant lands from
him who, by his cruelty and infidelity, had
trampled out her wedded love, and consigned
her to a living tomb.

With such conflicting thoughts as these
did Trelawney descend the hill, pausing as
he did to admire the ivy-covered ruins of
the old ancestral castle of the Montacutes.
There it lay at the foot of the hill, a picturesque object. There were the remains
of armorial bearings rudely carved in granite
over the principal entrance: a great white
eagle with wings extended, and the motto,
Je monte au ciel. A portico of granite

columns still remained in tolerable preservation, with great massive oaken doors, and numerous window traceries. The sight was a depressing one: those grey deserted ruins on that bright summer morning— the powerful family who once ruled there quite extinct; all their glory and greatness, their loves and their hates—all dead, and buried, and forgotten! and a stranger to their name and blood in possession of that castle and land, for so many generations the proud heritage of the great Montacutes.

Trelawney turned away with a sigh, and was going down the fine avenue of oak trees which still survive amidst the ruin of the family and their castle, when he was accosted by a smart dapper-looking man, who announced himself as the person who rented Montacute from the absentee proprietor, Lord Pengerseck.

" You have been looking at the ruins,

sir, I suppose," said Captain Sam Bennett. "Rather pretty, ain't they? But they take up a sight of good ground. I want the steward to get me permission to take them down. But my lord won't hear of it, though he scarcely ever comes down here."

"Why should you take the ruins down? they are a great ornament to the place."

"Well, as far as that goes, to my mind, sir," said Captain Sam, with easy familiarity, "a shaft sunk there, just where those useless old pillars stand, with stamps and a tidy counting-house, would be much more ornamental to the place, and a sight more useful. And then look at these fine trees, sir, we haven't any other such trees about here. Why, what splendid pumps they would make, and supply us with all the wood we should require both for the mine and counting-house."

"Who is the steward?"

" Mr. Treugrouse, sir."

" And is he in favour of pulling down the ruins ? "

" Oh, he doesn't care about it one way or the other, he always says when I speak to him about it. Only that I must leave the ruins alone, until such time as my lord gives permission to remove them."

" Which I don't expect will be either in your time or mine."

" Maybe not, maybe not," said Captain Sam, with nonchalance. " Some people are so bigoted and fond of their own way. You are our new parson, sir, are you not ? I heard you yesterday at the little church."

" Do you attend there regularly ? "

" Sometimes, that is if I like the parson. The last one was but a poor stick in the pulpit, and not worth going to listen to."

" Indeed, I thought he had been a very excellent man."

"He was well-meaning enough, poor man, I daresay, but he never could get to the root of the matter. I remember his trying to persuade me that sprinkling a little water on a child's face did it some good. That was when me and my missus wanted him to come up and give our little boy a name. He made us actually bring him to the church, he was that bigoted."

"Are you a Churchman yourself?"

"Well, I go anywhere, sir, I can get good. I generally go to the little chapel in the village. There is less form and ceremony. However, I don't say but I may look in on you now and then." And with this consolatory assurance, the little mine captain took his departure perfectly satisfied with himself, and with a jaunty motion of his finger towards his hat.

CHAPTER VI.

MR. TRELAWNEY'S FLOCK.

"But it is time," thought Trelawney, "to descend from my solitary heights, and get into the world again. If anything is to be done with this wild place, now is the time to do it. I am young, and strong, and active, why not throw myself into the work? 'Let the dead bury their dead,' wherefore dwell upon the past? It is irremediable. My predecessor lost heart about the place— could make nothing of the people, nor they of him ; so, come, I'll make the effort at any rate ! I have a good Cornish name to

begin with." So thought, so resolved, Trelawney, as he came down from Montacute
Hill, and after he had parted with Captain
Sam. The prospect was not an inviting
one, either locally or morally, look at it
how you might. Once you had quitted the
Montacute demesne, and its still considerable
plantations, and you found yourself in the
midst of desolation; great heaps of refuse
in every direction, as if all the rubbish in
England had been shot out in the place.
Mine chimneys dotted here and there, as
far as the eye could reach, and shabby
rickety-looking counting-houses with their
little balconies, from whence the work was
let out to the miners.

A tree was now a rare object, and those
that did grow in the neighbourhood were
almost all stunted ashes, bent from the effect
of many a westerly gale. The clay-built
cottages more resembled Irish cabins than

anything else; with this difference, however, that few of them were without their
bit of garden ground where myrtles, and
fuchsias, and geraniums might be seen all
the year round, and attaining a size which
we look for in vain anywhere but in Cornwall. It is Gudgodah, a "land of waters"
too: you are constantly coming to little
streams, and "stamps" where they wash
the tin. All day long may you see those
dark-eyed Cornish maids, with their picturesque sun-bonnets, busily employed in
this way. Such was the view which presented itself daily to Trelawney, as he looked
out of the windows of his picturesque parsonage, built to be in keeping with the
little early English church at no great distance off, in the most approved Gothic style.
It was quite an oasis in the desert was that
pretty little parsonage, with rose-trees climb-
ing up all round the windows, and clematis

and honeysuckle hanging in rich clusters about the porch. A well-kept garden, too, and flower-beds, bright with geraniums and heliotrope, and verbenas, gladdened the eye of the owner of this little paradise. While right in front of you was that lofty, majestic, unchangeable hill which had looked down upon so many generations, and which, as the lights and shadows rested upon its side, assumed so many varying appearances.

But now what of the people? what of that little flock in the wilderness whom Trelawney had come to tend? As may be said also of their own country, when you open your mouth to disparage, some redeeming trait presents itself, and checks your utterance. Blessed with an insatiable and ever extensive curiosity about your affairs, yet are they equally communicative of their own, and habitually civil and courteous in their demeanour. Fickle as their own climate, they are only too easily led after any novelty. The Cornish mind, like the Welsh, is eminently a religious one. They sing hymns and carols ("curls"), instead of the drinking and amatory songs wherewith the peasantry in other parts of England refresh their spirits. You may often come upon a "young youth," standing in the middle of the road singing a hymn at a loud pitch, either as a trial of his voice, or to summon his companions, rather than as a religious exercise, and he is sure to be joined by other youths before long, who make the welkin echo with their melody. For the Cornish, like the people of Lancashire, are fond of music, and whether in church, or going to "bal," or returning home from the mine, naturally betake themselves to this source of recreation. There is little drunkenness amongst the miners. Coffee and ginger-beer are the two beverages most in demand. But still it must be said of the Cornish miner that only let him sing "curls" to his heart's content, and he does not want any other species of "refreshment." It would be well if all this psalm-singing, and chapel-going (for church-going is decidedly the exception and not the rule in Cornwall,) commended itself by the ordinary tests of morality which we are in the habit of applying. But it must be allowed, as in the kindred case of the Welsh, that female virtue is at a remarkably low ebb among the mining girls and farm servants, and is seldom indeed ever to be met with. However, we are not writing a history of Cornwall, or its inhabitants. Enough has been said to give the reader, who perchance has never been in Cornwall (he would be called a "foreigner" down in those western parts—for the inhabitants often speak of themselves, and still oftener are spoken of by others, as if occupying some island, or dependency of the British Empire, and not as forming part and parcel of Great Britain),—enough has been said to give the non-Cornish reader some idea of the place and people whither Reginald Trelawney's fate had brought him.

The first thing to be done was to visit the people—to make their acquaintance : an embarrassing thing enough for a naturally shy, sensitive man like Trelawney—a man dropped down from the clouds it might seem to the people—to make his way unasked into their houses—to have to talk to them as if known to them all his life. There was no occasion for embarrassment, however. They were one and all delighted to see him. Those who were out when he called would when he met them beg that he would call again as soon as possible. Any member of the family who was absent

would deplore it as a personal misfortune.
So far so good: only they all seemed to
be under the impression that some wonderful piece of good fortune was to accrue
to themselves individually from the coming
of this stranger. Their glee, it must be
admitted, was that of children, or of some
primitive coloured tribes at the appearance
of a white man amongst them. They
would watch the stranger curiously, and
his going out and his coming in, and re-
peat with laborious precision anything that
had dropped from him, and speculate upon
his intentions towards themselves, and regard with admiring awe anything remarkable in his dress or proceedings at all.
This only until they got familiar with his
presence. Afterwards they would treat him
with as little ceremony as the savage who
whips his idol when it doesn't come up to
the mark—when it doesn't send the rain,

or food, or whatever it is the worshipper requires.

And then how they *did* crowd into that little church of Montacute for the first few Sundays after Trelawney came! Why, there was no getting a seat! and the little Bible Christian place over the way was quite deserted. The eagerness, too, of the people to listen! and how so many would stand up in order to hear better! Some even would come and sit on the pulpit steps, so as not to miss a word. It was most gratifying. And then the display of musical instruments! Nebuchadnezzar's collection was nothing to it—flutes, bass viols, violins, serpents, what not. It was a perfect ovation the arrival of this new parson!

"Who says that the Cornish are all dissenters?" thought Trelawney to himself each Sunday as he walked back from church for the first month or so after his arrival. "A better church feeling than there is in this place seemingly cannot be. And there was Captain Sam as usual in his place. It is certainly gratifying, after hearing so much of the emptiness of the church before I came."

Something of this sort would often cross through Trelawney's mind, as each Sunday witnessed the same overflowing congregations—the same eagerness to hear—the same hearty crowding about the clergyman (only there was a trifle too much of it) as he came out of the church, and made his way towards the gate. He was, however, greatly disgusted one fine Sunday morning, when he had taken more pains than usual, too, about his sermon, to find the church almost entirely empty—musicians and all disappeared—and to learn, as he soon did from the sexton, that *a woman* was preaching at the chapel, and that the people had all' gone to hear *her*. And his mortification was not by any means lessened when, upon passing the chapel (as he was unfortunately obliged to do), on his return from church, he was encountered by throngs of people flocking out of the meeting-house; some laughing and talking; some carrying . home their musical instruments swathed in green baize; and two or three throwing a careless nod of recognition towards their clergyman, and then jostling past him. Captain Sam: was amongst the throng, and accompanied Trelawney on his way home as long as their roads lay together.

"A capital sermon we have just had," he said, "from Miss Trotter. How she did give it to you parsons! I was thinking of poor Mr. Roberts all the time. 'Dumb dogs,' these were her very words, 'loving to slumber, lying down.' She said that they thought of nothing but their tithes

and their fees; and that if she had her
way a. person should have as much right
to choose his parson as his shoemaker or
tailor. We don't pay a shoemaker, she
says, if we don't wear his shoes; and why
should we pay parsons if we don't go to
hear them, or want to ? I thought she was
right there. It must come to people
choosing their own ministers, she said,
and the parsons would have to try and
please their congregations better. Don't
you think so, sir ? Now, why should I
have to pay tithes to Mr. Praed—a man
I never spoke to in my life, and who
wouldn't know me if he met me on the
road to-morrow? But I am keeping you,
sir. I should like you heard Miss Trotter
for yourself. How she does knock the dust
out of the cushions ! She preaches again
this evening, and I am reckoning you
won't have much of a congregation. Good
day to you."

CHAPTER VII.

RETROSPECTIVE.

IN the meantime the movements of the two ladies at St. Knighton's cottage were sedulously watched and reported on to the village conclave. Nor was this eagerness to find out something about them at all diminished, but, on the contrary, it received a considerable accession, when it became known that orders had been given by the steward who had the management of the St. Knighton property, that no persons should be allowed to trespass in the valley; and that, except in going to and from the mill by the direct path, no persons whatever were to be allowed to enter it without a written permission from him, and notices to this effect were duly posted. Of course, as we have said, this but stimulated the curiosity of the villagers, and others; and many was the surreptitious visit paid in consequence to the neighbourhood of the cottage, especially after dark, and many were the concealed eyes which took notice of the ladies and their habits. Not much, however, could be gleaned even in this way. To the daring intruders who continued to peer in through the window shutters on those grey autumnal evenings, when the ladies had come in from their walk, when they had lighted candles, and had shut themselves in for the night, no other spectacle usually presented itself than that of two ladies sitting quietly at their work or reading. The communication carried on between them was by signals, though occasionally she who was apparently deaf and dumb was able so far to articulate sounds as to attract her companion's attention when necessary, and even in some degree, as it would seem, to make known her meaning.

The history of the younger of those two ladies was plainly a sad one—she, I mean, who might be seen at times with her head leaning upon her hand, and buried in reflection ; or who—sometimes it was within doors, sometimes in the course of her walk —might be seen convulsively pressing her handkerchief to her eyes, and seemingly overcome with sorrow. At such times would her companion approach her, and with inarticulate sounds and gentle dumb caresses try to assuage that grief which passed utterance. The only person who ever crossed the threshold of the cottage after the ladies took up their residence there was the person who washed for them, and who lighted the fires in the morning, and did what simple cooking was required. But the ladies were almost as much a mystery to her as to others. The younger of the ladies she seldom saw, and the few directions she received from the other were usually conveyed in writing—two or three words, perhaps, written in a large clear hand. It was remarked that no names were written in any of their numerous books which were supplied from time to time to them by a neighbouring bookseller (who had his orders from Mr. Pearce), and that from their table and bed linen, as well as from their own body linen, the name had been carefully cut out. All, however, was of the finest quality, especially that which belonged to the younger of the two ; and there was no stint of anything which might be necessary for their comfort.

It is time now to say something respecting the past history of these two ladies, and of the link which connected one of them with Trelawney.

Of the elder of the two—Mary Wilson—little need be said. She comes upon the stage merely as the companion—the devoted, lifelong, attached companion—of the unfortunate, beautiful, highly-born Isabella Arundel. The daughter of a clergyman of small income in the north of England, Mary Wilson had yet no expense spared upon her education, in order to cultivate her mind, and render her accomplished. It was hoped in this way to alleviate the great privation of speech and hearing she laboured under, and to enable her to earn her own bread when her natural protectors should be taken away from her. She united with great quickness of perception and natural ability a loving, gentle, amiable disposition, and was remarkably unselfish and even-tempered. Thus it happened that, when a short time after the

deaths of both her parents, it was proposed
to her to go as a companion to the unfortunate Lady Arundel, who was then in a
species of confinement in her husband's
gloomy castle in Northumberland, she did
not refuse, but, on the contrary, flew to be
of any service and comfort she could to that
much-wronged lady, who, first as Isabella
Bertram, and afterwards as the wife of one
of the richest commoners in England, had
for a time appeared such an object of envy
to the country clergyman's daughter, whose
residence was at no great distance from
Bertram Hall, in the same county.

Isabella Bertram was the only child, by
the first marriage, of the representative of
one of the oldest families in Northumberland—Mr. Bertram, of Bertram Hall. Her
father, though keeping up a large establishment, and the nominal owner of an extensive
estate, was in reality an impoverished man,

and had only been enabled by repeated mortgages of his property to keep up appearances in the county. The principal mortgagee was Sir Edward Arundel (of the great banking house of Arundel and Treleaven), who resided chiefly in London, but paid occasional visits to his seat in Northumberland. Sir Edward was, in fact, the real owner of Bertram Hall, and it was entirely optional with him when to call in the mortgage money.

After Mr. Bertram, who was still in the prime of life, had remained a widower for several years, and after his only daughter was grown up, he contracted a second marriage, which, if it somewhat relieved his embarrassments, by no means tended to promote his domestic peace. For the second Mrs. Bertram, who was a handsome, showy-looking woman, and who soon gave promise of offspring, had from the very first mani-

fested an antipathy to her step-daughter,
and expressed a desire to see her married
off. At first there appeared to be every
prospect of a speedy fulfilment of her wishes,
for a sort of engagement had for a long time
existed, with her father's knowledge, between
Miss Bertram and the only son of the Rev.
Edward Trelawney, rector of Trelawney, the
adjoining parish to Bertram. The match
was considered a suitable one by all parties.
The families were of equal respectability,
and both of long standing in the county.
And though Mr. Trelawney himself was not
what could be called a rich man, yet his
brother in the same county was a man of
large fortune, a bachelor, and somewhat
advanced in life; and to his property of
five or six thousand a year was Reginald
Trelawney, Edward Trelawney's only son,
for a long time considered the heir. He
was brought up almost entirely at Trelawney

Castle, and never dreamt of a profession, unless a little amateur soldiering be one, for he had a troop in the Northumbrian Yeomanry Cavalry, and during a part of the year was styled Captain Trelawney, and wore his regimentals at the Newcastle assemblies.

Here it was he first met with Isabella Bertram, then just come out. Hanging upon her father's arm, and glittering with diamonds which had been her mother's (who was an Osbaldiston), she attracted general admiration, and was the belle of the evening. Reginald Trelawney, the heir presumptive to the family estates, was *somebody* in the eyes of Mr. Bertram, and of the maiden aunt who accompanied them to the ball as Isabella's chaperone. His attentions, therefore, were received with a good deal of satisfaction by the family; and, as he was to be met with everywhere in the county, at balls, in the hunting field, at reviews, wherever the élite of Northumberland were brought together, the wise ones were not long in predicting it would be a match. Nothing seemed more natural. And though Miss Bertram was fond of admiration, and would gladly have enjoyed her liberty a little longer, yet she not unwillingly fell in with the general idea that Reginald Trelawney was to be her future husband; and it was not long before he declared his passion, and was accepted conditionally upon suitable settlements being made by the uncle. Hitherto everything had gone on smoothly enough, and, now that Isabella had a stepmother, and one too much of an age with herself for them to get on very well together, there was an additional reason why the marriage should not long be deferred.

But what was everyone's consternation at Bertram Hall one morning, when a letter was received by young Trelawney, who was staying in the house at the time, from his uncle, and dated Cheltenham, informing him that he had been married that morning to the youthful and accomplished widow of one Captain Byrne, whose acquaintance, it subsequently appeared, he had made about a fortnight previously, having been struck with her pretty face, rendered still more interesting by a widow's cap, and the air of dejection she still bore on account of the demise of the gallant captain not quite twelve months previously.

This unexpected event made a great alteration in young Trelawney's prospects. It would be necessary, he perceived, at once to direct his attention to some profession, though rather late in the day for a man turned of five or six and twenty. It was true that his uncle expressed a hope that what had occurred would not have the effect of disturbing in the slightest degree

the affectionate intercourse that had so long
subsisted between them, and even conveyed
a message from the late Mrs. Captain Byrne,
to the effect that she hoped he would still
make the castle his home; yet still it was
too evident that things could not go on
as they had done, and that his expected
inheritance had probably passed away from
him for ever. For the relict of the deceased
captain was by all accounts a fair comely
woman to look at, and in the bloom of youth,
which, now that she had cast off widows'
weeds, shone out conspicuously once more,
as in the days when she had captivated
Lieutenant Byrne, of Her Majesty's 101st
Regiment of Foot, in her father's house
at Castle O'Rourke, on the banks of the
Shannon. There was every probability,
therefore, of a house-full of children at
Trelawney Castle: a probability, it may be
remarked, in passing, that in due time was

amply fulfilled; so that, what between the children she bore to Mr. Trelawney, and what between the frequent visits paid by one or other of the five Miss O'Rourkes, occasionally varied by the stay of one óf her brothers, the house was never empty again during the remainder of Squire Tre- lawney's days.

Something of this sort was foreseen by young Trelawney, and so accordingly there seemed nothing for it but to fall back upon the family living of Trelawney, which, upon his father's death, had been destined for his old tutor, Mr. Wayte.

Beyond a natural disappointment, Isabella Bertram did not care much for the change in her intended husband's fortunes. She was too devotedly attached to him for this; and, if the truth must be told, she was too desirous to get away from her stepmother to be willing to remain at home any longer

than she could help. Besides, was not
Trelawney rectory said to be worth 600*l.*
a year, and that would come to them one
of these days no doubt? that is, so as none
of the little Byrne-Trelawneys wanted it.
And, then, had not Reginald two or three
hundred a year of his own—his mother's
fortune? Altogether Isabella was quite prepared to marry upon what they had got,
and what they had in prospect. Luckily
her stepmother seemed to take the same
view of the matter, and even undertook to
talk her husband out of his objections,
when an unlucky incident altered the whole
state of affairs, and completely crushed the
young lovers' hopes. What that was, we
proceed to narrate in the next chapter.

CHAPTER VIII.

SIR EDWARD ARUNDEL.

It will be remembered that Sir Edward Arundel, the London banker, was the principal mortgagee of the Bertram estates. Sir Edward, who was sprung from a younger branch of the "great Arundels," as they used to be called in Cornwall, (where the family was originally settled), was a man of middle age, and had the reputation of being a person of extremely immoral habits. He had taken to banking when a young man, and had amassed such a large fortune as to be able to become the proprietor of the family place, with a portion of the estates, of the earls of Northington, in Northumberland, very near the border. Here he resided during a portion of the year in a species of rude magnificence; his visitors being mostly "fast men" from town. For his society was not courted in the county, and it would have been impossible for any married man who respected himself to sit down to table at Northington Castle with the mixed company, both male and female, whom he was sure to meet there. Even Mr. Bertram, though he knew himself to be at the banker's mercy, never visited at the castle, and had no intercourse with Sir Edward, except in the way of business. Indeed, the reports of his profligacy, and of the doings at the castle, were such that there were some magistrates who could not be prevailed upon to sit on the same bench with him; and more than once it was rumoured that a case of affilia-

tion brought against the baronet would have
to be decided on by the justices who acted
for that part of the division in which
Northington was situated. It was curious,
too, that one who was known in town principally as an excellent attentive man of
business, and who lived so decorously, as
far as the world knew, at his splendid
mansion in Eaton Square, should, when in
the country, exhibit such a total disregard
to public opinion, and revel in every species
of debauchery.

A grim satisfaction was it to Sir Edward
to know that he had Mr. Bertram, and one
or two other county magistrates, at his
mercy. By a very short process, he might,
in all probability, have made himself master
of Bertram Hall, as he had of the place
which he now called his own. And if he
didn't exercise this power, it was rather
because it seemed to give him increased

consequence in the county—the knowledge that he had this power—than from any feelings of mercy and humanity, to which he was a total stranger. Though not visited at his own house, or to be met with at any houses of mark in the county, yet Sir Edward occasionally made his appearance at county balls, and on occasions of that sort was usually accompanied by some of the more respectable portion of his visitors from the castle. And it was at one of these balls, and very soon after she came out, that he first met Isabella Bertram.

Sir Edward was a man of too much con-sequence to be overlooked altogether, and there was always this feeling respecting him uppermost in the minds of prudent mammas, and even of the young ladies themselves, what an admirable catch he would be—with his title, and fine place, and large fortune! Besides, he was a man of refined tastes as

respects literature and the arts, and his
manners were peculiarly fascinating. Altogether it was the fashion to speak of him
with some degree of leniency, and many
were the damsels who only desired to have
the opportunity (lawfully secured to them)
of seeking to turn this great sinner from the
evil of his ways, and to win him back—
supposing he had ever trod them—to the
paths of virtue and purity. Sir Edward
had no difficulty then in securing as a partner any girl in the room he fancied, and
it needed only to have it made known that
he had parted with some of the extremely
undesirable inmates at Northington Hall,
and meant to reform, to have every house
in the country thrown open to him, and to
be in a position to see county society at
his own spacious castle.

Isabella Bertram at once attracted Sir
Edward's notice, and she had too much girlish

vanity not to be pleased at her conquest.
Any serious thoughts about him she had not,
for though not actually engaged to Mr.
Trelawney (himself by no means a despicable
catch), yet she could not be blind to his attentions, or to what they would probably end
in. But when she noticed Clara Forster's,
or, again, Henrietta Musgrave's evident gra-
tification at having obtained the baronet as
a partner, and could even overhear the
former's praiseworthy efforts to engage Sir
Edward in something like improving conversation, it must be admitted that Isabella
Bertram could not resist showing, in the
eyes of the ball-room, what she *could* do
if she had a mind. Accordingly, much to
Trelawney's disgust, Sir Edward was allowed
to enjoy a larger share of Miss Bertram's
lively conversation, and bright animated
looks, than her lover approved of.

It did not require much of Sir Edward's

sagacity to perceive how matters really stood between Trelawney and the brilliant Isabella Bertram. But he was too much a man of the world to make any public display of his feelings, or to seek to enter into open competition with such a formidable rival—who had youth on his side, and the advantage of a previous intimacy. Sir Edward knew he must go to work in a different way to oust his rival, whom he already thoroughly disliked. Contenting himself, therefore, with having made an obviously favourable impression upon both father and daughter by his quiet unassuming manner—so different from what might have been looked for in a man about whom such stories were told, and who was reputed one of the richest commoners in England,—Sir Edward gracefully withdrew and left the field in possession of his younger rival, who seemed inclined to assert

a sort of right to Isabella's hand, and safe
keeping.

A gentle reminder from Sir Edward's solicitor that the interest payable half-yearly by
Mr. Bertram had been due for some time,
with an intimation that, "if perfectly con-
venient to Mr. Bertram," Sir Edward would
be glad to call in the mortgage money, as he
had a large purchase to complete,—a letter
to this effect having reached Mr. Bertram at
the breakfast-table one morning not long
after the meeting with Sir Edward at the
Newcastle ball—by no means tended to
promote the cheerfulness of the party as-
sembled at breakfast. For gloom is infec-
tious; and it was quite certain, both to
Isabella and her stepmother, that that busi-
ness-like looking letter written on blue paper
contained something the reverse of agreeable to Mr. Bertram. His face wore an air
of anxiety for many a day afterwards, and it

was soon known to his wife and daughter
that some money transactions between himself and Sir Edward were the cause of his
disturbance.

Misfortunes proverbially never come alone,
and it was just at this juncture, when
Mr. Bertram did not very well know which
way to turn himself, that the news arrived
of Squire Trelawney's unexpected marriage
at Cheltenham. And this necessarily led to a
review of his daughter's engagement to Reginald Trelawney. Anything that the young
man had, must come to him after the death
of his father, who was far from being an
old man, and in the meantime the young
couple must live principally upon any allow-
ance which the two fathers could make.
This, in Mr. Bertram's case, and under
existing circumstances, would be merely
nominal. Even his daughter's moderate
fortune of 4,000*l.* was "locked up," as her

father expressed it; which meant, in plain
English, had been spent by himself, though
ultimately secured on the estate. Altogether
Mr. Bertram viewed with much distaste his
daughter's engagement with Trelawney, now
that he was in a manner penniless, and
anticipated from it nothing but demands for
money which he was in no position to
comply with.

It was about this very time, that Mr. Bertram was surprised one morning at receiving
a visit from an old hunting acquaintance
whom he had seen little of for years, and
his intimacy with whom indeed had been
principally confined to the field.

Being accidentally in the neighbourhood,
was referred to casually as the cause of the
visit, and an invitation to stay and dine
was readily accepted. Nothing was thought
of it, and Mrs. Bertram was only too glad
that some one had dropped in to dissipate

the *ennui* of the dinner-table.   Left alone
with Mr. Bertram when the ladies had with-
drawn, and after a preliminary glass or two
of port, Mr. Osbaldiston, who was a namesake, but only a very remote connection of
the first Mrs. Bertram, broke ground by
saying in a careless sort of way,—

"Your daughter, Bertram, has sprung
up into an uncommonly fine handsome girl
since I last saw her.   I once thought her
a little too dark, when she used to ride
after the hounds ; but, by Jove ! you seldom
see such a fine girl now.   She was the
admiration of the whole room, I can tell
you, at the last ball.   By the way, do you
know that Sir Edward quite lost his heart
to her ? "

" Sir Edward Arundel ? "

"Yes : why we don't boast of any other
Sir Edward in the county, unless it be that
old gouty fellow, Sir Edward Blackett, our

Member. I thought Reginald Trelawney seemed very sweet upon your daughter that night, Bertram. Excuse me, but I have a reason for asking you—is there an engagement between them ? "

" There *was*," replied Mr. Bertram, dryly.

" Ah, poor fellow ! since his loss of fortune, he must think of something else beside marrying. Now listen to me, Bertram, what I have got to say to you. I have come over this morning all the way from Northington Castle, where I have been staying the last week."

Mr. Bertram moved uneasily on his chair, looked hard at his guest, and then filling a glass of port, and pushing the decanters towards his friend, prepared to listen to what Mr. Osbaldiston had to say.

" It is about your daughter I have come to speak. I have told you how Sir Edward admires her. But the fact is, he has heard that she is engaged to Reginald Trelawney, and, before stirring in the business, he wished me to ascertain whether it is so or not. I understand from you that the engagement is at an end ? "

Mr. Bertram nodded assent.

" Indeed, nothing else could be expected since old Trelawney has gone and made such a fool of himself. Now, Bertram, you know very well that Sir Edward Arundel is not a young man—not exactly the man whom you could expect to see coming over here gallivanting after your daughter (who is twenty years at least his junior), perhaps to be rejected after all, or to have that black-muzzled fellow Trelawney—who, between you and me, gives himself a confounded deal too much airs—to have him thrown in his teeth. You couldn't expect it, I say. So what does Sir Edward do— he is as honourable and straightforward a

man as you could wish to meet—but he
commissions me to come over here and
make out how the land lies. 'Osbaldiston,' says he, 'you are an old friend of
Mr. Bertram's :'just go over, and if there
is no engagement with that fellow Trelawney—and I hear it is broken off—do
you go and ask Mr. Bertram's permission
for me to come over and cultivate his
daughter's acquaintance, with a view to
making her an offer of my hand. I have
been gay in my time,' he said, 'but I wish
to turn over a new leaf. When one is no
longer young, Osbaldiston,' he said, 'one
gets tired of the sort of life I have been
leading, and if I could only meet with an
amiable accomplished young lady who would
have me, and teach me better, why, I should
consider myself a fortunate man. Money,
you know,' he said, 'is no object with
me; and Isabella Bertram'—he knows her

name, you see—'would adorn a palace.'
Now I have told you, Bertram, exactly
what passed between us, and you must
decide on what answer I am to bring back
when I leave here to-night."

" Take a bed here, Osbaldiston, and I
will give you an answer in the morning.
This is a thing that requires to be well
weighed."

" Well, it is a long drive back to Northington, sure enough—a good twenty miles,
if it is a yard; and so if Mrs. Bertram
will give me a bed I'll stay, and hope to
bring back a favourable answer to Sir
Edward, for he is as keen as any young
lover after your daughter. When a man
of his age falls in love, he is up to his
neck and shoulders in no time."

" What about all those women and loose
fishes Sir Edward has had about him at the
castle ? "

"All to be got rid of, upon my word and honour. They are to get the sack directly; not that I know anything against them myself. Indeed, when I have been staying there, nothing could be better behaved than they all were. People talk a great deal, Bertram, about the goings on at the castle; I can only say, I never witnessed anything wrong or improper there in my life. There used to be ladies certainly sitting at table with us, but who they were I never asked; I never did, if you will believe me. They used to take their glass of champagne and enjoy themselves, but I never saw anything wrong about one of them in my life; I never did, upon my honour."

"Come, let us go upstairs, Isabella will give us a cup of coffee."

CHAPTER IX.

THE PROPOSAL.

MR. OSBALDISTON'S mission was so far successful that he was able to bring back a message to his principal that Mr. Bertram would be glad to receive a visit from him whenever it was agreeable to himself to come. It was thought better to keep Isabella Bertram entirely in the dark as to the object of Sir Edward Arundel's visit. She would naturally connect it with the business transactions which, she was aware, had passed between him and her father. The engagement between herself and Reginald Trelawney she looked upon rather as in abeyance, than as being entirely broken off. For, though obliged to turn to a profession, and though possessed of but limited means for a time, yet it was quite certain that, upon the death of his father, he would be the possessor of a competency —small, indeed, when compared with what he had looked forward to, or with what the daughter of Mr. Bertram might naturally have expected, but still enough for all reasonable purposes of comfort and enjoyment. Isabella Bertram, then, cherished the hope that difficulties would disappear, and that she might yet be the happy wife of Reginald Trelawney. He had, indeed, left home for some time to complete his terms at Cambridge, and to read for orders.

No objection was made on the part of Mr. and Mrs. Bertram to an occasional correspondence between Isabella and her lover; for none could be insensible to the great hardship of the young man's lot, and to the cruel reverse of fortune he had sustained. However, it is, we fear, human nature all over to take a dislike to persons in misfortune, and to avoid them, as the deer do their wounded fellows. From being first an object of very sincere sympathy at Bertram Hall, Reginald Trelawney and his change of prospects ceased after a time to interest either Mr. or Mrs. Bertram; and the subject was tacitly dropped. Though it was known that Miss Bertram occasionally heard from him, yet no interest was expressed as to his plans or present occupations; and if this was the case before Mr. Osbaldiston's visit, we may be quite sure it was still more so after it.

For Mrs. Bertram espoused Sir Edward's cause with a degree of interest from the very first, and she was only restrained by tact and prudence from giving open expression to her sentiments. Her indifference to Trelawney, then, very soon turned into open hostility, and one of her very first proceedings was remorselessly to consign to the flames, unopened, one letter after another which Trelawney had addressed to his intended wife, and to pursue the same course with respect to Isabella Bertram's letters to him. This was not long in producing its effects upon her stepdaughter, whose listless gait and absent look betokened that all was not going on smooth between herself and her lover; nor did she ever suspect, until long afterwards, the wrong that had been thus done her. Not even Mr. Bertram himself was aware of it. It happened thus very naturally that Mr. Trelawney's name ceased to be mentioned in the family; and, as it was pretty well known that his father

was of opinion that a handsome young
fellow like Reginald might do better than
tie himself to the daughter of a struggling
man like Mr. Bertram, who was sure to
involve in ruin all belonging to him, Isabella had no one to turn to for sympathy,
either in the one family or the other.

Such was the state of things when a
visit from Sir Edward was announced one
morning at Bertram Hall, and the announcement, for the reason given before,
caused little surprise, and did not seem
to afford any interest to Isabella. In
every country-house, however, an agreeable
visitor is an acquisition, and such was Sir
Edward, eminently. He was equally attentive to all, and did not by his manner
indicate any special preference or admiration for Miss Bertram, beyond what cour-
tesy and good breeding would suggest to
any gentleman in addressing a young and

beautiful girl. Sir Edward soon fell into the way of the family, and though occasionally absent at Northington, or having to run up to town upon matters of business, yet at Bertram Hall he seemed very much to have established himself; and whether it was talking politics to Mr. Bertram (who, like himself, was a staunch Tory, while it was well known that all the Trelawneys were strong Whigs), or amusing Mrs. Bertram with *on dits* of the clubs, or seeking to form Miss Bertram's taste in works of art, of which he was a connoisseur, he contrived to make himself equally pleasant and agreeable to all. Nor were excursions to Northington, and one or two other old Border castles of interest in the neighbourhood, which Miss Bertram had never seen, wanting to give variety to the visit, and to make the days pass pleasantly.

All this time, the thought of Sir Edward

as a lover never entered Isabella Bertram's mind. He was quite as attentive to her mother as to herself, and was old enough to be her father; and it was only after Mrs. Bertram had one day expressed an anxious desire that Sir Edward might make her an offer of his hand, and had dwelt upon how it would be the " saving" of them all if he would, that Isabella Bertram was led to bestow a thought upon the subject. Her first impulse was to reject such an idea with indignation. She would despise herself, she thought—and she said as much to her stepmother,— if she was to forget in such a short time the man to whom she had given her heart, and *that* merely because he was no longer heir to a large fortune: she wouldn't hear of such a thing, she said.

Mrs. Bertram didn't think it wise to oppose her daughter's resolution too strongly. She

said little about it at the time, but would
every now and then recur to the subject,
and give Isabella to understand that the
making or the ruin of the family was pretty
much in her hands.

"You do not understand, perhaps, my
love," she would say with a tenderness of
tone unusual to her, "that your poor father
is a ruined man if Sir Edward insists upon
his rights. He has only got to call in the
money he lent your father, and this place
must pass out of our hands, after having
been in the Bertram family for generations.
We should have to leave the place, and
what would become of us all I really do not
know. It is quite natural, my love, that
you should wish to marry Reginald Trelawney—that is, if he is willing to marry
you; though they *do* say that he has fallen
in with some girl of large fortune in the
south, and wishes to marry *her*. I don't

know whether this is true, perhaps not ; but we all *do* know that the father, Mr. Edward Trelawney, is averse to his son's marrying you ; and this he makes no secret of. However, as I was saying, my love, though you naturally first think of your own happiness, and Reginald Trelawney's too, yet you will not, I am sure, forget your poor father altogether, and how deeply he is interested in your not refusing Sir Edward, should he make you an offer; which is almost more than I dare hope for. I say nothing about myself, and your little sister. We have of course no claims upon you as your father has; and I am afraid, dearest Isabel, that you have never been very fond of your stepmother."

Constant dropping will wear the hardest stone, and by degrees Isabella Bertram found herself weighing what was to be said for the other side, as well as on the side

which had hitherto enlisted all her sympathies.   The long silence of Reginald was
perplexing; and it certainly was rumoured
that he was paying a good deal of attention to a young lady in the neighbourhood
where he was reading with a tutor.   More-
over there was the dislike of his own family
to the connection; owing a good deal, it
was said, to the political differences which
had always kept the two families apart, and
prevented any intimacy between them.   Then
there was the point her stepmother was so
often referring to : If Sir Edward pleased,
he could turn them all out of their home !
And if the Trelawney family were averse to
the match now, what would it be when they
had lost their standing in the county, and
had not a roof to cover them ?   Reginald,
too, was proud.   Was it quite certain that
he would keep his engagement after it was
known that the family was ruined ?   And then

her father! would he survive the disgrace? Probably not,—and all to be averted, all to be set right, if I only give up thinking so much of my own happiness, and am willing to make some sacrifice? If Reginald really cared for me, he would have written long before this. Would it in reality grieve her to be quietly released, and by my own act, from an engagement which neither of the families approve of? And then, woman-like, Isabella's thoughts would turn upon the splendid demesne, grand castle, and extensive establishment, which would call her mistress, were she to accept Sir Edward's hand in case he made her an offer. It was some time before Isabella got accustomed to such a train of thought, but once the alternative presented itself to her mind, she found it difficult to get rid of it.

At length the crisis arrived; she must make her choice. From her father she learnt that Sir Edward had spoken upon the subject, which he declared was nearest his heart, he had offered princely settlements, promised the devotion of a lifetime.

Mr. Bertram was not a man of many words, but in making this communication to his daughter, and in preparing her for the interview which her lover sought with her, he gave her to understand that the offer had his own cordial sanction, and that he trusted his daughter would well weigh the consequences to them all before she rejected it. Sir Edward's manner was all that Isabella could have desired—tender, and considerate for her feelings in his tone, while there was a manly self-reliance, and independence in what he said. He spoke of the time when he first saw her,—of the admiration she then excited in him,—of what appeared at the time, the hopelessness of seeking to engage her affections, as they had been already bestowed,—of the obstacle removed, as he had been informed, that he was not a young man, he knew,—was perfectly conscious of his unworthiness to aspire to the possession of such a treasure,—but if the devotion of a lifetime, the tenderest care for her happiness, would make amends for disparity of years, and wipe out the recollection of many failings,—would she deign to accept the hand which in all humility he offered her? The struggle in Isabella's mind lasted but for a few moments,—something inarticulate escaped from her, a burst of tears relieved her, and a tender gentle embrace from Sir Edward followed. She left the room as his affianced bride.

CHAPTER X.

THE WEDDING.

A VISIBLE air of satisfaction pervaded the house when it was known that Isabella had accepted Sir Edward. Mr. Bertram's cleared brow, and a warm embrace from her step-mother, assured Isabella of their approval of what she had done. And though there had been no express stipulation upon the subject, yet a tacit understanding there was, that Isabella's acceptance of Sir Edward was to be followed by some effort on the part of the latter to put Mr. Bertram's affairs straight, by means of pecuniary accommodation which

was at the banker's command. Nor was Sir
Edward slow in fulfilling this expectation.
For during one of his temporary absences,
Mr. Wenlock (his solicitor from town) paid
a visit to Bertram Hall, by the desire of
Sir Edward; the object of which was to
make an arrangement that would be satis-
factory to Mr. Bertram. Accordingly, by
advancing money at a lower rate of interest
than Mr. Bertram was paying, Sir Edward
enabled him to get rid of some of his more
troublesome creditors, and to leave himself
a wider margin of income to live upon. The
purchase by Sir Edward of some of Mr.
Bertram's unentailed property, at a figure
considerably above the market price, contributed still further to his relief. And
altogether Mr. Bertram found himself, for
the first time in his life almost, (for the
estates were encumbered when he came into
them), comparatively a free man,—that is,

his only creditor was his future son-in-law, and from him annoyance was not to be anticipated.

The preparations for the wedding were pushed rapidly forward, as Sir Edward wished to take his bride upon the Continent while the fine weather lasted, as the season was now pretty far advanced; and the day in October was already fixed upon when Isabella was to bestow her hand upon him. There was plenty to keep up her interest in the meantime;—a visit to be paid to town in order to select her wedding dress, and to be furnished with her *trousseau;* carriages to be inspected in company with her lover, and numerous consultations held as to what additional furniture would be required for his already handsomely furnished houses in town and country. Time sped rapidly thus employed, and Isabella— with an occasional pang, certainly,—was becoming more and more reconciled to the prospect before her. Her composure, however, was destined to be disturbed; for upon the very eve of her wedding-day, and as she was taking a last solitary walk through the Bertram plantations, she was suddenly accosted by a man in the dress of a groom, or stable-helper, who, after ascertaining that she was Miss Bertram, placed a letter in her hand, and then disappeared.

A thrill, prophetic of the contents of the letter and of the writer, ran through Isabella's frame, and compelled her to sit down on a rustic seat at hand, before she could summon up courage to open the letter, or do more than glance at the address. It was in the handwriting of Reginald Trelawney, as she expected. She opened the letter at length, and read as follows:—

"I do not write to reproach you, Isabella, for your breach of faith, much less to seek

to win you back again. You have inflicted
the greatest wrong upon me, which it is
in a woman's power to inflict. I have
borne loss of fortune, total change of prospects, even the indifference of friends, but
all was as nothing to me as long as I believed that my Isabella was faithful. Even
when you ceased to answer my letters, I
trusted you still. I could not believe it
possible that you—you who hung upon me
but a few months ago, in such an agony
of grief at our parting—you who pledged
a life-long constancy—who said that nothing
in this world could ever alter your affections,
or induce you to forget me—that *you* could
now be guilty of such an act of incredible
heartlessness and cruelty towards me.

"Oh, Isabella! I said I would not reproach
you, but it is hard not to do so. You have
spoilt all my plans and purposes of life
by the part you have acted. Only a week

ago, upon my return to England after spending a couple of months reading with a tutor in a remote part of France, I was rejoicing in the brighter prospect that seemed to be before us, for I found a letter awaiting me from Sir Henry Throckmorton, offering me the rich living of Ossulton as soon as I was capable of holding it. And then, on that very same day, this dreadful news reaches me, that you have forgotten all your vows and promises, and are going to wed a man whose character for immorality has been such, that no respectable persons would have him inside their doors. What infatuation has possessed you? Is it merely the vulgar attraction of title and wealth, and a large establishment? Do you suppose that the man who has so long lived with the most depraved and worthless—both of your sex and mine—can at once alter his nature? can at once throw

off his life-long habits of sensuality? No!
Mark my words, Isabella! from a long knowledge of this man's character, I know that
when he is tired of his new plaything, he is
capable of remorselessly casting you off, and
returning to those habits of indulgence in
which he has so long lived. But I check
myself. This man may be already your
husband, or just about to become it. If
I have wronged him, no one will more re-
joice at it than myself; but if I have not,
remember that, as long as life lasts, you
have in me one who would gladly die to
be of service to you.

" What is to become of myself can hardly
now interest you. It is impossible for me
to go and live at Ossulton, which is, as you
know, the parish church of Northington.
I cannot make up my mind to be a witness
—necessarily a frequent witness—of your
married life, be it a happy one or the

reverse. I shall go to a distance in preference,—it may be to my own far away county, there to remain until such time as in the course of nature I succeed to Trelawney.

"And now farewell, beloved Isabella! Cruelly as you have acted, it is impossible I can ever forget you—ever be indifferent to you. Remember the great love I have borne you, and how I have cherished it amidst the disappointment of my expectations, and all the trouble and anxiety which that change necessarily involved. Farewell, beloved one! Think sometimes of one who was never unfaithful to you even in thought, and who even now in the hour of desertion and misery, desires your happiness beyond everything else in this world.—REGINALD."

Isabella read this letter in an agony of grief. It seemed to revive every scruple and foreboding that had ever been in her mind respecting this marriage. And then

her cast-off lover—her once fondly loved
Reginald—what a heart must she have,
to have forgotten him even for a moment?
All his losses and disappointments were
surely hard enough to bear,—but now to
find himself deserted by one he had loved
so well, to whom he had been so constant:
for did he not speak of letters of his un-
answered?—and this at a time, when all
seemed coming right again! With such
bitter thoughts as these was Isabella's mind
filled as she returned to the house.

What an effort it was to remove all traces
of her grief, and to clothe her face with that
brightness and with those smiles which are
looked for in a bride elect. And then there
were cousins, and aunts, and friends of the
family, arriving at the Hall for the ceremony
next day; all to be greeted with kindly
welcome. To all must she exhibit a smiling,
happy face, while her heart within her was

full of bitterness and remorse. It was in vain that she pleaded to herself her father's distressed circumstances, and the sort of necessity laid upon her to sacrifice herself in order to relieve them. It would not do. Something very like perjury did it seem to her, to vow to "love, honour, and to obey" one for whom, she knew, she could feel but little affection, and still less reverence. But it was no use, she felt, indulging in such thoughts—they came too late. The sacrifice must be made ; and, accordingly, putting by Reginald's letter, to which she in vain attempted an answer, and shedding a few last bitter tears over it, Isabella Bertram prepared herself for next day.

The ceremony was to be performed quietly by the rector at the parish church, and in the presence of a few near friends and relations of both families. Sir Edward arrived at the church from Northington in his car-

riage and four, accompanied by his friend
Mr. Osbaldistone, at exactly ten o'clock,
and in a few minutes afterwards three or
four carriages were seen approaching the
church from the Hall containing the bridal
party. The service was performed as usual;
the books were signed; and the whole party
conveyed back to Bertram Hall in the same
order as they came, only that now the bride
and bridegroom led the way in Sir Edward's
carriage. There was the usual breakfast;
the customary healths were drank; there
were the same dreary attempts at wit, ordinarily exhibited on such occasions, but which
fall still-born from the perpetrator, and are
felt by him and all the guests to be palpable
failures. Then there was the general rising
from table; the leave-taking of the supposed
happy pair, who were setting off for the
Continent.

But we hurry over these details to get

back all the sooner to those two deserted women at St. Knighton's Keive. For one of them—she with the pale, placid face—was a looker-on at the ceremony on that wedding morning—had gazed with admiration on the bride's beauty, and half envied her the brilliant lot that seemed to be before her. While the other — she with looks which sorrow had touched, indeed, but not marred —she was the bride of that eventful morning, resplendent in beauty, the admired of all. Little could it have been foreseen that the calm, attentive husband, who took his place by Isabella's side in the carriage, and waved adieu to the crowd of well-wishers at the door, was to be the stern, implacable tyrant of future, and not very distant days; to be his wife's relentless gaoler, the author of her life-long misery!

Not much was heard of the married couple for some time, beyond an occasional brief announcement of their plans, as they moved about from one place to another on the continent. For there was no one at home to whom Isabella could write confidentially. Her father was, of course, out of the case; and there was not that sufficient cordiality between her and her step-mother to invite confidence on either side.

At length it was known that Sir Edward and Lady Arundel had arrived at Northington, and a few formal visits were exchanged between them and the surrounding families; but, from some cause or other, there was little intercourse of a sociable kind kept up. Sir Edward was away in town a great deal upon business, which had fallen into arrears in his absence, and it was soon rumoured that he was so jealous of his wife as to have forbidden her to go into society in his absence. Certain it is, that Lady Arundel seldom stirred from the castle grounds except in her husband's company. Was it that they were so devoted to each other, or what was it? The intercourse kept up with Bertram Hall was slight, considering the near relationship of the parties, and neither side manifested any eagerness to increase it.

It has been said that Lady Arundel seldom paid visits in Sir Edward's absence; but an unfortunate exception to her rule which she made, about twelve months after her marriage, paved the way for all her after troubles. This was a morning call which she paid at Throckmorton Park, some six or seven miles distant from Northington; and here almost the first person she encountered upon entering the library, into which she was shown, was Reginald Trelawney, who was staying on a visit at the Park. As no one was in the room at the time but himself, the meeting was embarrassing enough; but the awkwardness soon wore off. No

allusion was made to the past, and the conversation turned chiefly upon Continental
topics with which both were familiar. After
some little delay, Lady Throckmorton entered
from the garden, and seemed at first in no
small degree alarmed at the chance meeting
between the two former lovers. However,
as they appeared to be conversing together
calmly enough, the subject was dismissed
from her mind, and after a time a walk in
the garden and through the conservatories
was proposed, until luncheon was ready.
Here, unluckily, they were joined by several
other visitors, with none of whom was Lady
Arundel more than slightly acquainted; so
that, as a matter of course almost, she fell
to Trelawney's care, and before long they
found themselves somewhat separated from
the rest of the party. There was a silence
at first between them, which Reginald at
length broke by saying—

" Are you happy, Isabella ?"

A hasty " Yes; as happy as I could expect," was the reply.

" Well, we must be good friends, and try and forget the past," went on Trelawney. " Were you very angry with me for my letter? I wrote it in great trouble and bitterness, but I am afraid I did not think enough of your feelings at the time."

" Well, Reginald, your letter certainly did pain me very much at the time, and has so since; and I have sat down more than once to tell you so. Oh, if you could have known all, you would not have reproached me so ! I never received any of your letters, and so I thought you had forgotten me; and then your father said he did not wish us to marry —and there were other reasons for acting as I did, which I cannot explain to you. Do you forgive me, Reginald ? I know how very, very badly I have acted towards you;

but oh! do forgive me! I have been so unhappy!"

" Dearest Isabel, I may not tell you all I have gone through on your account—all I have suffered from your desertion: that is past and gone. But believe me, that you have been dearer to me than my own life; and that to my latest hour I will cherish the remembrance of the love that once subsisted between us."

A flood of tears was Isabella's only answer for some time, but at length she said—

" I am very sensible of your consideration and forbearance. I know how much I have wronged you, Reginald. Try and forget that such an unhappy person as myself ever crossed your path!"

A servant at this juncture announced that luncheon was ready, and Lady Arundel, after composing her feelings as well as she could, and, accompanied by Trelawney, rejoined the rest of the party.

This short garden scene had not, however, altogether escaped the eyes of the rest of the party, nor were the traces of Lady Arundel's tears so carefully removed, but that they attracted some degree of notice. The servant, too, who had been sent in search of Lady Arundel had witnessed quite enough of her ladyship's agitation to be able, with embellishments of his own, to regale the Arundel servants with gossiping surmises at their mistress's expense; which, as it afterwards appeared, they were not slow in propagating.

CHAPTER XI.

THE FALSE STEP.

SIR EDWARD was still absent in town. It was a week after the drive to Throckmorton Park, and Lady Arundel had had ample leisure to brood over what had passed between her former lover and herself—for visitors were few and far between at Northington—when the post brought one morning a note, which she at once recognized to be in the handwriting of Trelawney. It was as follows:—

" DEAREST ISABEL,

"Do not be angry with me, if I seek one more interview with you. I am leaving this part of the country for a long time, and going to reside in Cheshire as chaplain at Cholmondeley Hall. Now, do not refuse me. I must wish you a long good-bye. We may, perhaps, never meet again. But I feel as if I could not be happy without once more seeing her whom I have loved so well, and with whom I had hoped to have spent my life. I shall be to-morrow at the Obelisk at about four o'clock, and you will not refuse to meet him whom you once called your own

" REGINALD."

Lady Arundel paused long over this letter. Pity, and recollections of old times, prompted her to comply with the request; but prudence whispered No! What had passed at Throckmorton occurred through no fault of hers. The meeting was unexpected on both sides. But *this* would be something deliberate—a clandestine meeting with one not her husband—with a former lover. It was a thing that, if discovered, must ruin her in her husband's eyes. She knew herself to be surrounded with spies.

Unfortunately, she had not insisted upon a total change of servants upon her marriage; for, though the upper servants were all new, yet many lingered about the place in subordinate situations, who had been accustomed to Northington under the old régime, when it had been ruled by mistresses, and the taint of the past seemed still to infect the household. What necessity, then, for circumspection! How many would be glad to make mischief between husband and wife!—how many had an interest in seeing some deposed mistress take her place once more in the household! And then her husband!—who so exacting, so cold and unrelenting as he was? What would it be for such a thing to reach his ears?—he so suspicious and jealous, as it was, especially against this very Trelawney! She felt she could not dare to brave his fury in case of a discovery. The knowledge, too, of her own unprotected, friendless state, and of the obligations her father was under to him, seemed to have hardened him against her. And then his disappointment at there being no prospect of an heir—this seemed to have extinguished whatever little affection he might ever have entertained for her, and to have inspired him with something like hatred. His return home was never looked for by his wife but with uneasiness. The usual suddenness of it, too, seemed to indicate suspicion, and his departures for town or elsewhere were equally unceremonious.

Lady Arundel was at a loss how to act. She could not bear the thought of refusing

Trelawney the last request he was ever to make of her. She reflected upon his unvarying tenderness, his unselfish consideration shown towards her at all times, and the unmistakeable grief he exhibited just lately for his loss of her. No, come what might of it, she would give him one last meeting —say one word of kindness and farewell, and then forget him for ever—devoting herself ever afterwards faithfully and honestly to fulfil her husband's wishes.

Accordingly, four o'clock came, and found her approaching the Obelisk (erected in memory of one of the Earls of Northington), situated on a gentle eminence which formed the back-ground of an extensive wood, about half a mile distant from the Castle. Here she found Trelawney awaiting her.

"I fear I am doing a very indiscreet thing," she said, "in giving you this meeting. But I could not bear to refuse you. Oh! Reginald, let it be our last meeting—if my husband were to hear of it, I am undone: and you will not detain me. I can never tell when Sir Edward may not return: it is always without notice, and he has been away now for some time."

" Dearest Isabel, not for the world would I risk your happiness. It has been inconsiderate of me, I fear, to ask you to meet me. But, oh! my love!—my first, and only love,—I cannot leave this country—perhaps for years—perhaps never to see you again—without saying one word of farewell to you—without telling you that the remembrance of what you have been to me, will accompany me to the grave."

They had descended by this time into the wood, and had walked as far as the point where the paths diverge—one conducting direct to the castle, and the other leading to the main road. The few last words had been spoken, and with a bursting heart Isabella was turning away from Reginald, unable to suppress her emotion any longer, when her eyes encountered the stern fixed look of her husband!

In a voice of thunder he asked his wife, "What she did there?" and then turning with looks of fury towards Reginald he cried, "Begone, sir, out of my sight! Is it thus you dare to tempt my wife from the duty she owes to me? Leave my presence, sir,—you are upon my land. Your remaining is a fresh insult to me. No; not one word, sir, shall I hear out of your mouth. What I have seen, what I have heard, is enough." And with these words Sir Edward turned away in fury from Trelawney, who in vain endeavoured to address him, and pursued his way to the castle by a different path from that which his wife had taken.

Sir Edward's fury was, if possible, increased rather than diminished, when he entered his wife's dressing-room upon his return to the castle. He loaded her with every term of reproach that occurred to him,—upbraided her with the benefactions he had conferred upon her father—threw in her face her interview with Trelawney at Throckmorton (which had been communicated to him in an anonymous letter written by a female hand), and declared that from that hour she should cease to rule at Northington. He even insulted her, a few days afterwards, by intruding on her presence a showily dressed female, who, it was well known, had formerly lived with him as his mistress, and when Isabella's indignation could no longer restrain itself, he even dared to lift his hand to her.

This was too much to bear. In the course of the day Lady Arundel was missed, and it was soon discovered that she had walked down to the village, and, having engaged a fly, had been driven in the direction of Bertram Hall. Sir Edward was soon in pursuit, and reached Mr. Bertram's within a couple of hours after his unfortunate wife.

Her reception there had been far from encouraging. The recital of her wrongs met with little sympathy, either from her father, or step-mother, while the mention of her two interviews with Trelawney, and her explanation of the circumstances under which they occurred, drew down upon her a storm of reproach and even invective. She was accused of being insensible of the obligations the family were under to Sir Edward, and indifferent to the probable consequences to her father of the step she had taken,— unless that step were instantly disavowed. The carriage should be ordered, then, and back she must go to Northington. Mr.

Bertram would not for the world that she should sleep out of her husband's protection for a single night.

Matters were in this state, the carriage had been ordered, and poor Isabella was considering where she could fly for refuge from her husband's cruelty and violence,—since even her own father cast her off—when the arrival of Sir Edward put escape for Isabella out of the question. In a stern voice he demanded whether it was with Mr. Bertram's sanction he found his wife there? Was her father aware how she had acted towards him in his absence? His wife should return that instant with him, or never more set foot at Northington. Mr. Bertram was only too anxious to assure his indignant son-in-law of his own and Mrs. Bertram's high disapproval of their daughter's conduct, and volunteered post-horses, that no delay might take place in sending Lady Arundel

back to her home. Thus, was the luckless
Isabella denied sympathy or shelter at her
father's house, which she had quitted a short
time before a seemingly happy bride. And
it was long before her last long look of
despair—or the remembrance of her fixed,
set features—faded from her father's memory; for he never saw his daughter more,
whom he had once loved so fondly: nor did
Isabella Arundel ever again cross the threshold of her father's house !

The little that was known of her after
she had been brought back to Northington,
was this:—She was strictly confined to a
particular part of the house, and for a
long time was denied intercourse with any
human being. Even the servants were forbidden to speak to her, or to answer her
any questions, while a small garden close
to the house was assigned to her for purposes of exercise. The most rigorous orders

were issued against any person approaching
Lady Arundel when taking exercise. So
far was this carried, that an old labourer,
who had worked for a good half century
upon the estate, was discharged upon the
spot for holding the garden-gate open for
Lady Arundel as she passed through it, and
saying, " God bless your ladyship."

Only once did Lady Arundel ever meet
her husband again, and that was when
accident brought him past the hurdle-gate
which admitted into the garden where she
was in the habit of taking exercise. It so
happened that at the very moment Sir
Edward was passing, this little gate opened,
and he and his wife stood face to face—the
first time for several months. Sir Edward
stood for a moment, as if uncertain what
to do, while his wife's altered looks seemed
to stab him to the heart. But unhappily
for Isabella Arundel, the lady who had taken

her place in the house, was at Sir Edward's elbow at the moment, and saying the words, "Remember your promise, Sir Edward," drew him away.

Soon after Christmas, it was Sir Edward's custom to leave Northington for some months, and to occupy his town house, and then it was intimated to Lady Arundel by the steward, in writing, that she was at liberty to walk about the grounds wherever she pleased, only that she must submit to be kept in sight by one of the under-gardeners. Another indulgence, she was informed, had been sanctioned by Sir Edward, namely, that she was to be allowed the companionship of a young lady, a little older than herself, the daughter of a clergyman lately deceased in the neighbourhood of her old home. But as this lady,—though highly accomplished and reputed to be of a most amiable character,—was almost born deaf and dumb (the effects of scarlet fever in child-hood), it was doubtful whether Sir Edward, in consenting that she should live as com-panion to Lady Arundel, was not actuated quite as much by a species of refined re-venge, as by any motive of pity or con-sideration for his unfortunate wife. Under the plea that his wife was suffering from extreme nervous excitement, bordering on derangement, Sir Edward contrived to keep at bay all troublesome visitors, and to silence the inquiries which her father could not avoid addressing to him from time to time.

A twelvemonth was passed by Lady Arun-del in this species of confinement at North-ington; at length, her husband, wearying of the restraint which her presence in the same house during a great portion of the year imposed on him, or having satisfied himself with revenge in this particular way—

or perhaps afraid, from the report of her altered looks, that she would die upon his hands, and that this might lead to an investigation of the circumstances under which she was kept in confinement—suddenly conceived the idea, which he was not long in putting into execution, of having his wife, with her companion, transported to one of the wildest solitudes in Cornwall.

How he carried out his purpose our readers are already aware. The answer respecting Lady Arundel was, that it had been found necessary to place her under some degree of restraint in the south of England, but that with perfect quietness a restoration of her health might be looked for; that she had every comfort, and the companionship of a clergyman's daughter (rewarded by an ample salary). With this explanation every one, including her father, professed to be satisfied. Nor was

it until something like the truth, though
not the entire truth, became known, that
public indignation in his own county, and
elsewhere, was drawn down upon the head
of Sir Edward Arundel and his advisers.

CHAPTER XII.

CORNISH PEOPLE—A SKETCH.

WE now return to Montacute and its Incumbent, whom we left rather disgusted, if the truth must be told, at the sudden desertion of his entire flock, drawn off by the counter attraction of the meeting-house. The problem that every newly-arrived clergyman has to solve, when he undertakes a charge in Cornwall, is to devise some means of winning the people back to the church; of *fixing* them once more in the faith of their fathers. For, notwithstanding their love of novelty, and a certain fickle-ness of disposition and proneness to act from impulse, (which they have in common with other Celtic people), none have adhered more steadily than they have to their religious faith, or have given more repeated proofs of their zeal and constancy. For—to go back to a very remote period, indeed —where did Druidism take such a strong hold as among the ancient Britons of Cornwall? Look at the numberless Cromlechs, Holed Stones, Logan Rocks, Druidical circles still to be found in this (as it might almost seem) enchanted land; the natural home of giants, whose traces in the shape of enormous, fantastically-shaped stones, meet the traveller's eye throughout the entire of the Land's End district. Or—to come to a later, though still a very remote period. (the time when Christianity was first preached to the ancient inhabitants of Cornwall by devoted missionaries from the Irish shores)—

observe the numberless crosses erected,
especially throughout the west, to com-
memorate the event,—observe how almost
all the parish churches are named after
these men of God, in grateful commemora-
tion of their labours! What a revolution
in men's minds in these remote regions do
not these things witness to! What a zeal
in replacing the human sacrifices once offered,
it may be, on that very stone, which stands
yonder upon pillars in the midst of the moor,
by the unbloody offering of the Christian
altar !

And when Christianity, in this form, had
taken firm root in the Cornish mind, and
had abolished Druidism with its cruel rites,
where did the ancient Catholic worship
linger longer amongst the people, and retain
a firmer hold over their minds than in this
very county, where now it can hardly be
said to have a footing ? Long after the

Reformation had been firmly established in other parts of England, the sacrifice of the Mass continued to be offered up in many a Cornish church, and the clergy still acknowledged the authority of the Roman Pontiff.

Then to pass over a century and a half, when Wesleyism had its rise, who more stoutly resisted it ?—who more valiantly stood up for the faith of their fathers, than these same Cornish miners ? But it was all in vain. Methodism broke in like a flood. It met, it may be, some craving of the Cornish mind, which had slumbered for ages since the overturn of the ancient faith. At any rate, it spread, and now covers the land.

And so that devotion which once showed itself in magical circles, Logan Rocks, and Holed Stones through which to drag their children, and which in succeeding ages led the Cornish to erect their noble granite churches, and name them after their deliverers — to cover western land with holy crosses, and to make pilgrimages to the holy wells of St. Madron and St. Uney, and, when called on, to fight fiercely for the creed of their fathers and for the ancient Catholic worship, and which in succeeding ages made them rise up as one man to expel the emissaries of schism from their ocean-washed shores—that devotion now expends itself in Revivals and Camp-meetings.

The parish churches in west Cornwall, as a rule, are deserted by the descendants of those who fought so stoutly for them, and whose remains are mouldering under the shadow of many a lofty grey tower.

As we have said, Trelawney was not a little disgusted at the sudden disappearance of his flock, and began very much to qualify the favourable opinion he had at first formed

as to the state of Church feeling at Montacute. He had not, indeed, come down into
the country with any pet project of his own,
and proclaiming that all that his clerical
brethren had been hitherto doing was "a
mistake" (as some have been known to do);
that, only try *his* plan, and all would be
right again. No: he had a much humbler
opinion of himself and of his own attain-
ments; but still, he thought that earnestness
of purpose, and steady work in his new
parish, would tell in the long run. But he
began to fear he was mistaken. The Captain
Sams, and the Captain Dicks, of his neighbourhood had a vested interest in the little
whitewashed meeting-house. It was their
own property; they made money by it.
None must hope to be employed in the
mines under their command, unless they
attended the meeting-house and contributed
towards its support.

The Church might do well enough for great people and the parson's own family, but the meeting-house for the people—that was their own, and they wanted no other! Such were pretty much the sentiments which Trelawney heard daily echoed amongst the miners and mine captains whom he encountered. The interest they took in the Church or its prosperity might be represented by a very low figure indeed. It was, indeed, a more respectable place to be married at, than the meeting-house, or registrar's office : that was allowed. There was some lingering notion that it might be just as well to bring their children, and get them "named" there ; and the church-yard was certainly the usual place to bury in. Here begin and end pretty much the Cornish miner's notions of the use of the parish church, and its appendages.

And then the clergyman, he is with them,

emphatically, *the* gentleman of the place—
a person to touch your hat to, and to " sir."
He may be a bit of a doctor, or a bit of
a lawyer, and if so, his medical, or legal
skill, is sure to be in frequent requisition.
Anything irregular, anything contraband,
for the Cornish miner.   He has much more
faith in the parson's medicine, than in the
doctor's drugs, and would sooner consult
him any day; and that not merely to save
expense, but from a real belief that " parson
knows more about it than t'other."   And
the same with law, or business of any sort;
the Cornish peasants invariably prefer the
parson as an adviser, to any regular prac-
titioner.   But let it be about a matter of
theology, of religious " experience," of
clearing up some difficulty in Scripture, and
the parson is the last person the Cornish
miner will think of coming to consult.   No,
the village cobbler, the mine captain, the

called Ding-Dong,) said to have been worked
by the Jews ages and ages ago; and say
what can exceed the awful solitary grandeur
of the scene !

Many then were the sociable out-of-door
parties which Trelawney was invited by his
hospitable clerical neighbours to join; frequently it was in the company of his friends the
Tressilians : not great monster gatherings
were they, where one half the party is
scarcely, or not at all, acquainted with the
other half; but really friendly, sociable meetings, where the main object is, not so much
to eat and drink—though that is not to be
overlooked, either—but rather to scramble
about the rocks, to stroll along the shore, to
pick up shells and sea-weed, and to have a
pleasant chat with the fishermen or their
wives. Or, it may be, that you have a fancy
to stretch yourself—with a companion by your
side, or, book in hand—on the gorgeous

purple heath, with its many shaded blossoms, or on the smooth, short turf, and to think of the time when you were young, or in love, or when last there, and with whom: good, kindly, soothing thoughts, which you feel all the better for having dwelt upon. Thoughts which draw together in spirit the absent and estranged; which soften the most worldly heart, inspiring it with tender recollections of the past, and do not fill it with gall and bitterness, or waste themselves in useless, unavailing regrets.

Such is one good in *pic-nics*. You do not go to eat and drink merely; you take just enough of everything that is pleasant and good, in order to promote cheerfulness, and would then do well to abandon yourself to the enjoyment of the coast scenery, (for all the pic-nics in Cornwall are to some favourite rock, or headland), listen to the soft ripple of the waves lapping the rocks

at your feet, or feast your eyes—say upon
yonder fairy-land, with its serpentine spires,
and columns, and pinnacles, all glittering
in the sun, and resplendent in colours of
green, and red, and purple; or listen to
the merry ringing laugh which proceeds
from yonder group who are adventuring to
the extremest westerly point of England.

Some such thoughts must have been
passing through Trelawney's mind as he
lay at length upon the smooth, short turf
which overhangs Pardenack Point—the most
remarkable, with one exception, of all the
headlands about the Land's End, and which
has been immortalized by Turner's pencil.
The rest of the party, consisting as it did,
of Charlotte and Loveday Tressilian, and
two or three of the juvenile members of
the family, with a couple of young ladies
on a visit at the rectory, were scattered
about the rocks, sketching, or in pursuit

of samphire, or exploring dark caverns in pursuit of maiden-hair fern, or what not.

"How one could dream away one's life here!" exclaimed Trelawney; "so far from the turmoil of life; with these unchangeable rocks all about one, and the tides perpetually ebbing and flowing. How glorious would be a storm here with the spray dashing up over these gigantic rocks! Where was it I was reading lately that all between this and Scilly yonder was once a fair and beautiful land rich and fertile, but that the sea broke in upon it and swept all away?"

"Exactly so, sir; that's very true," said a voice close beside him. "There is no doubt about it. There *was* such a country; and me and others have many a time, when out fishing, pulled up the remains of windows, and doors, and planctions."

The speaker was a hardy, bronzed-faced old fisherman, carrying an empty basket upon his back, and apparently making his way to the little fishing village of Sennan Cove, a short distance further on.

"Sit down here, and tell me something about it: but first have a glass of ale." Complying with both these invitations, the hardy old fisherman took his seat on a piece of rock close by where Trelawney was.

"Have you got any of those windows, and doors, and floors, you speak of, or where are they to be seen?"

"Bless you, sir, I have something else to do than to be keeping such things by me. They be of no mortal use to any one. They were old-fashioned looking enough to have been some of the fittings of Noah's Ark; but what's become of them, I can't rightly say. They have been made away with somehow. But you see, sir, there, where the

Scilly Islands are in the distance, right before us. Well, it is said that once upon a time there was a fine country between this coast and those islands, and plenty of houses, and as many as a hundred and forty churches. But that one night a great flood arose and covered the whole country, and swept away all those houses and churches. Only one man escaped, and he was the ancestor of Squire Trevelyan. His horse swam ashore, and he upon its back."

"Yes, I know, and that is why the Trevelyan family have a white horse rising out of the sea as their family arms."

"Yes, sure, the same as is over the inn door at Goldsinny. I have been there many a time and oft selling fish; and the rocks you see there in the distance, sir, they be at the top of the hills which are under the water. There be curious sights, sure enough, seen here by us fishermen; especially after dark."

" I should think so," said Trelawney dryly. " What are they?"

" You noticed, sir, that long strip of beach on the other side of the rock?"

" Whitsand, you mean—where we got this bag of shells?"

" The same.   Well, will you believe me, sir, I have many a time seen ghosts and spirits moving up and down the shore, and none of us fishermen dare go down there after dark—that is, alone.   If I have to go near it, I bring a little child with me."

" What for ? "

" To protect me; for ghosts never harm little children.   Even the coast-guardsmen don't much like going down there by themselves.   There have been so many wrecks off that part of the coast that it is believed

the spirits of those that were wrecked walk
about there still. I spoke to our parson
once about laying them, but he only laughed
at me. I wish the Werdron parson was
alive again; *he* was the man for laying
ghosts. Why, sir, if he wanted his horse
held, he had only to plant his stick in
the ground, and a spirit would rise up and do
his bidding. My father's greatgrandmother
has seen him do it scores of times. Why,
she minds the time when he raised a spirit
to appear as a witness at a trial, and the
cause was won, too, by that means. But
after the trial the ghost was not willing
to leave, and so the parson had to say the
Lord's Prayer backwards seven times before
he could lay the ghost. Ah, he was a
wonderful man, that parson!"

"Is there any smuggling or wrecking
carried on now, as there used to be?"

This question the old fisherman seemed

to have some difficulty in answering. But, after casting a shrewd look at his interrogator, and taking in by his dress a general notion that he was one of the quality, he went on, though in a lower key than he had used before:

"With regard to smuggling, sir, it is more difficult than it used to be. Not but that I know where a gentleman like your honour could be well served with real old French brandy and the best of tea, if you were willing to pay a moderate price for it. I think I know of a man who has got some to dispose of now. But your honour wouldn't peach?"

"I don't want any. But how is it managed?"

"Why, you see, sir, when a boat runs in with its cargo into any of those creeks along here, we are ready—or, leastways, there are some ready—with two or three

horses, and the tea and brandy are put
into panniers, and the horses are off in
no time. It is not often that we are
caught. They burn a blue light from the
shore to show that none of the coast-
guardsmen are about, and the thing is
soon done. It is more difficult than it
used to be, howsoever. I mind, when I
was a boy, that so long as we supplied
the officer of the coastguard here with
lots of brandy—he was a drinking, swearing
sort of chap—he would let us do as we had
a mind, and never took no notice of what
we ran ashore; except sometimes, for the
show of the thing, he would seize, maybe,
a keg or two only half filled, which
we had left purposely in his way. Why,
bless you, sir, in those times we supplied the parson and all, and old Mr.
Penglaze—that is grandfather to the present man — with all the brandy and tea

they mostly required. There is scarce an old house about here but you may see the hiding-places, where they used to conceal the things they got in this way, and by reason of mishaps at sea."

" There is no wrecking now, is there ? "

" You have hardly the chance given you. It is a shame; if the sea throws anything ashore, it is taken from those who have the best right to it, and carried off to Penzance, or to somewhere else, and I'll be bound little is heard of it afterwards. Those officers divide it snugly between themselves, they do say. Why, it was only last winter the shore was strewed with as fine a wreck as you would wish to see,— kegs, and barrels, and jars, and boxes, and what not, all knocking about, and bumping up against the rocks about a couple of mile from where we are sitting—round Cape Cornwall way, and forenent the Brisons:

it was *they* that did the job; but before a
poor man could gather up an armful of
things, and while the women were scrabbling
away and all was a mingle-cum-por, down
came those thieves of coast-guardsmen and
revenue officers, swoggering and cursing like
mad, and vowing they'd clunk us all up,
and have the law of us—I don't know
what they weren't going to do, and all
because we wanted to get a few bits of
things the sea had brought to us. I don't
hold with 'ticing ships on the rocks by
means of false lights, as they used to do
in my father's days—though he never saw
any harm in it, he said; but it is a shame
we should be deprived of all our rights as
we are now-a-days. But I must be jaleing
along. I wish you good-day, sir."

" Well, Mr. Trelawney, who has your
companion been ? " was Loveday Tressilian's
greeting as she scrambled up the rocks, and

stood beside him, flushed with exercise and the sea breeze. "Do you know Charley has been making a sketch of the fisherman? He looked so picturesque with his white hair floating in the wind. Who is he, and what can you two have been talking about so long?"

"He is an old smuggler, and he has been pleading for the practice of wrecking. Come, shall I go and order the horses? They must be refreshed by this time."

"That is what I came to say. Charley thinks it is time to go home." And so Reginald set himself to get his little party under weigh.

CHAPTER XIV.

LADY ARUNDEL'S LETTER.

SIR EDWARD ARUNDEL had not managed
matters with so much secrecy but that the
truth began to ooze out, not many months
after the hapless Isabella had been removed
to a distance. It is easy indeed, for a certain time, to baffle the inquiries of relations
by an ingenious mystification, by speaking
in grave measured tones of such a one
being under " medical *surveillance*," of
" disordered state of the nerves," " mental
excitement," " need of perfect quiet," " dislike to see any one,"—expressions and modes

of speaking which may mean anything, from the privacy of home to confinement in a lunatic asylum under the tender mercies of a "mad doctor." And though Sir Edward was an adept at such mystification, from long experience in the art, yet such were the rumours—the dark mysterious rumours— abroad in the county respecting his wife's fate—some affirming that she had been made away with—was dead, in fact, and others that she was in close confinement somewhere—that at length, urged by the remonstrances of friends of the family, Mr. Bertram made up his mind to call his son-in-law to account as to what he had done with Lady Arundel. A letter was accordingly written to this effect, and de-spatched to Sir Edward's address in town.

It was some time before any reply was received, and when it did come, it consisted merely of a few lines guardedly expressed, intimating that Lady Arundel was well in health, and provided with every comfort she could require; but declining to afford any further information. The writer concluded by stating that, as he was on the eve of starting for the continent, and as his movements would be uncertain for some time to come, any further letters must be addressed to him under cover to his solicitors, Messrs. Wenlock and Gooch, Gray's Inn.

As may be supposed, such an answer was far from allaying the anxiety that began to be felt and openly expressed as to Isabella's fate; and there is no saying what steps parental anxiety, now thoroughly aroused, might not have induced Mr. Bertram to adopt, when just at this time a letter was received from the unhappy victim herself. An aunt has been spoken of—her father's sister—and to her this letter was addressed.

As it is almost the only authentic account we have of the confinement this much-wronged lady underwent at the hands of her husband in Cornwall, it is thought proper to give the letter entire; only suppressing one or two passages in it, for reasons which will be obvious to every one.

August 19, 18—

"MY MUCH-LOVED AUNT CARY,—

"I AM afraid that you have been all very unhappy on my account for this some time past; and I would have written before only that I was under a promise not to do so, as the condition of being allowed to take exercise and to have what books we require in this most solitary of all spots. Siberia can be nothing to it, as *there* you have some one to speak to. But here from one week's end to another we never hear the sound of a human voice. I had almost

said we never see a human face, but that
a poor woman from some neighbouring
village comes every morning to light the
fires and make out the rooms, and to do
whatever is required—which is very little,
as our wants are but trifling. In our walks,
too, which seldom extend beyond this
valley in which we live, we have seen
persons intently watching us from a distance, and even imagine that at night
we are spied in upon through the shutters.
But this may be fancy; for, leading such a
life of seclusion as we do in this remote
shaded valley, through which the sun's
beams hardly ever break, you can imagine
how nervous and fanciful we both get.

"You may wonder why we do not address
ourselves to some of the neighbours, seek
out the clergyman, or some one of influence.
But we dare not, dearest Aunt Cary. The
only condition upon which Mary Wilson is

allowed to remain with me—and how tender and affectionate she is words cannot describe—is that she strictly conforms herself to the rules Ronaldson (Sir Edward's steward) laid down when he brought us here. And one of those rules is that we are not to address ourselves to any human being, either by letter or word of mouth, nor to receive any visitors. We are not to walk to the village, nor in any direction where there are houses, nor where we are likely to meet people.

"Upon observing these conditions, we have a good deal of liberty extended to us, and can be supplied with what books we please from a neighbouring town. Indeed sad as this sort of life is, it is one degree better than the miserable time I spent latterly at Northington, when daily insult (from which we are here happily exempt) was my sorrowful portion. And much, dearest aunt, as I yearn for home, and to see dear papa and you again (though he did let his poor Isabel be dragged away from her father's house), yet sooner than return to live with Sir Edward Arundel as his wife, or be confined in one of his houses, and daily insulted by the presence of those vile creatures he has about him, I would prefer remaining in this gloomy valley. Here, at any rate, I have peace. I am not much worse off than one of the nuns at Lanherne, whom we used to read of. *Their* imprisonment is for life—hopeless—and they cannot stir beyond the convent walls, and garden; but we can walk about here with tolerable freedom, and amuse ourselves with our books, and flowers, and needle-work.

This is better than violent altercations with Sir Edward; who spared no term of bitter reproach in addressing me, and would taunt me most ungenerously with having married

him merely for his money, while my heart
was really Trelawney's: indeed, upon one
occasion he struck me,—that was when he
discovered in my desk (which he had broken
open) a letter which poor Reginald had
addressed to me just before my marriage,
when he was very unhappy, poor fellow, at
my cruel desertion of him. There was
something about Sir Edward, I know in the
letter, which irritated him when he had
read it, and then unfortunately I had com-
menced answering it. Altogether we had a
scene, which ended, as I said, in his actually
striking me, and from that day forth, I
think he has hated me. And as for poor
Trelawney, his fury when he met him in the
wood that day, was something frightful to
witness. And then he had been told by
one of those wretched women who haunted
Northington, that I had given Trelawney
a meeting at Throckmorton, and was seen

alone with him there in the gardens,—altogether, he vowed he would never forgive me to the longest day he lived, and said that I should have bitter reason to rue my conduct.

" You know, dearest aunt, that it was by mere accident I met poor Reginald at Lady Throckmorton's, and chance threw us together in the gardens.   And then as for giving him a meeting at the obelisk on that unfortunate day, it was certainly very imprudent of me, and I know I oughtn't to have done it; but it was the last time, in all probability, I was ever to see him—so he said. I felt how cruelly I had used him, and how I had spoilt all his prospects ; and you know how fond we had been of each other, and that once it was all settled we were to be married, and papa and Mrs. Bertram were so pleased at it.   Altogether I could not refuse him one last meeting, just to say farewell for ever ; and we were about separating—and I

13—2

do not deny, aunty, that he held my hand in his, and was imprinting a last kiss upon it— when Sir Edward was upon us in a moment, and applied such words to me, charging me with wickedness of which I was entirely innocent, so that a reconciliation between us became, from that hour, an impossibility.

" Oh, dearest aunt Cary, my heart melts within me when I think of home, and of all that I have lost, and how happy I might have been with poor dear Reginald, if Mrs. Bertram had not interfered, and stopped our letters—as I know now she did. And then she worked upon my feelings about dear papa's circumstances, and said it was in Sir Edward's power to set them all right again : altogether I was over-persuaded to commit a great sin, for which I am now suffering bitterly, in vowing to be fond of a man whom I did not really love, and in casting off one who deserved better at my hands—who would have made, I know, a fond, tender, indulgent husband, and who would never have shut me up in this dark, gloomy valley, to die here, perhaps.

"And now, farewell, dearest, best beloved Aunt Cary. I was always your pet when I was a child, and when you used to stay at Bertram after my own dearest mamma's death. You will not forget your poor forsaken Isabella, imprisoned in this valley by that hard, cruel man, who has embittered my life. I dare not tell you where we are. It is only upon this condition that Mary Wilson has promised to enclose this in a letter to a friend of hers in London, so that it may be put into the post there ; and some time to-night, when it is quite dark, we shall steal down to the little village post-office, and put this letter in.

" Give my fondest love to dear, dear papa, and a kiss from me to little Emmy, my god-

daughter. My health is, on the whole, good;
though the dampness of the climate, especially in a valley like this, affects me sometimes. Farewell.

" Your own fond,

" Isabel."

Great was the emotion shewn both by
Mr. Bertram and his sister on the receipt of
this letter, and many were the plans dis-
cussed for finding out where poor Isabel had
been conveyed. There was only one clue to
it in the letter, and that might be purely
accidental—the allusion to Lanherne Convent in Cornwall. But, though a letter of
inquiry was addressed to the rector of the
parish in which Lanherne is situated, (which
proved fruitless), yet upon consideration
it was not thought that any importance
could be attached to the allusion, as in the
early days of Sir Edward's acquaintance,

Lanherne, and its convent, which had formerly been the seat of Sir Edward's
ancestors, used to form a frequent topic of
conversation between him and Isabella; Sir
Edward being in possession of some fine
engravings of the convent and of the
romantic valley of Mawgan, in which it is
situated. Application to Sir Edward's solicitors met with no better success than the
letter addressed to the rector of Mawgan.
They professed entire ignorance upon the
subject, and absolutely declined giving any
information respecting their client and his
affairs. Lastly, Miss Wilson's relations were
made out; but they could give no information either. A letter had been occasionally
received from her, but it had been invariably
dropped into the London Post-office, and so
forwarded to its destination. Indeed, when
it was known that, as a condition of the
handsome salary received by Miss Wilson,—

which enabled her to give a good education to several brothers and sisters who had been left slenderly provided for, and were in a great measure dependent upon their eldest sister's exertions—absolute secresy as to her abode was to be observed, it was not to be expected that any information was to be gained in such a quarter.

There was nothing for it, then, but to wait for another letter, which might be more explicit; or for Sir Edward's death, which, of course, would have the effect of terminating Isabella Arundel's seclusion from the world.

CHAPTER XV.

MISS WILSON'S LETTER—LADY ARUNDEL'S JOURNAL.

As throwing some additional light upon the narrative of Lady Arundel's sufferings, and her melancholy fate, it may be as well to insert here a letter which has been placed at the writer's disposal for the purpose of this narrative, and which would appear to have been written by Miss Wilson to a friend in London some months after she and her companion had taken up their abode at St. Knighton's. The cover bears the London post-mark only, so it is probable that, as

with Lady Arundel's letter, given in the last
chapter, it had been enclosed to some third
party who posted it. The letter now lying
before me, and which is written in a bold,
legible hand, runs as fellows, viz. :—

" DEAREST FANNY,
        " You will easily understand that
there are difficulties in the way of writing,
and forwarding a letter, from this *most out of
the way* place, which will account for my
silence. You know that the only condition
upon which I am here at all, is exact obedience to Sir Edward's orders ; and one of
those orders is, that I am to afford no clue
whatever to Lady Arundel's residence. Were
I to do so, I should deprive her of what I *do*
believe she clings to as her mainstay and
support under her great trial—that is, my
being with her ; while I should do her no
good by disclosing her place of residence. For

nothing would be easier than for Sir Edward
to carry her abroad, and shut her up in a
convent, or mad-house; or else, even in this
country, to bury her in some place equally
remote or distant as this—only without its
advantages.   These advantages are personal
liberty—freedom from molestation and insult, and a supply of most of the requisites
and conveniences of life, including a good
supply of books.

" You know, too, dearest, that in my case
there are other considerations not to be lost
sight of. My affliction makes one place much
like another to me,—as respects society at
least: indeed, I have a sort of morbid dislike to towns, or even to meeting people.
This has grown upon me since I have
been in this secluded valley: this much I
may tell you, as there are many ' secluded
valleys ' in England!   Though we hardly
ever see a creature, and in this way have

no variety, yet what between our walks—
we have once or twice even stolen down to
the sea-shore at night (what do you think
of that?)—and our books, and our drawing
and painting—(for you know how beautifully
Lady Arundel draws? and a good deal of
pains was taken with me in this way, and
no expense spared by dearest papa,)—what
between these employments, the time does
not hang so *very* heavy upon our hands.

" Lady Arundel is affection and tenderness
itself towards me, and I cannot, for one,
believe that she has done anything to de-
serve her husband's treatment of her. We
get on very well together, and can talk
almost as fast on our fingers as you and
I used to do when we were girls at school
together. Lady A—— has at times her
fits of weeping, and deep depression of
spirits. She will sit for an hour together
lost in thought, or walk up and down near

the cottage, seemingly in great trouble. I do
what I can to comfort her; but I think she
generally wishes to be left alone, and so I do
not intrude upon her grief, which is sacred
in my eyes. Often when I look at her,
especially when she is in trouble, I think of
the wonderful change in her circumstances—
from having been the mistress of a fine
house, with servants and carriages at her
command, now to be shut up in this little
cottage, with poor me for her sole companion, and only a charwoman to wait upon
us! Or, as I remember her, Isabella Bertram, a fine, handsome, spirited girl, fond
of riding, and so much admired by gentlemen at all the Newcastle balls; and now look
at the almost heart-broken Lady Arundel,
who keeps walking up and down hour by
hour as if chafing at her confinement and
longing to flee away and be at rest!

" The cottage we live in is too damp,

and the valley too much shut in by the hills and overgrown with wood, for either of us to enjoy good health. Lady Arundel's looks have altered for the worse since we have been here: she has lost almost all her colour, is very easily fatigued, and complains often of headache. As for me, I suffer more from rheumatism, and neuralgic complaints. However, on the whole we keep pretty well, so do not be alarmed.

"I do believe people here consider one, or both, of us—probably it is *me* from my scarcely ever speaking, and having to make signs—as out of our minds; they accordingly avoid us on all occasions (though this may be by orders), and eye us curiously from a distance. Lady A. is a great fern collector, and takes an interest in comparing the different varieties we have here—the *Asplenium marinum, Maiden's hair,* &c.

"And now I must draw this letter to a

close. What is to be the end of this
banishment, I know not. Lady A—— thinks
that it will only end with Sir Edward's life.
But this would be a sad prospect for us.
I don't mean Sir E.'s death, but having
to await that event before we can be set
free and return to the world. Lady A.
says she will forget how to speak soon, as
well as myself, if she remains much longer
here. And from the motion of her lips I
perceive that she is often talking out loud,
or perhaps repeating something. God help
us !—two poor forlorn women, cast out from
all human sympathy, and shut into this
valley ; it may be, for our lives !

" Ever your affectionate

—*May*, 18—   " MARY WILSON."

Except from these two letters, and from
a few scraps of writing in the shape of a
journal, which were afterwards found at

St. Knighton's, little can be known, now, of the interior life of that cottage. All that ordinarily met the eye, was the spectacle of two ladies, whose walks appeared to be principally confined to the valley and its precincts, but who have been occasionally met, or more frequently seen returning as if from some distant walk.

The strangest accounts were in circulation respecting their habits ; some affirming that they never addressed each other, while it was as stoutly contended by nightly eaves-droppers that not only shrieks and cries, but distinct words issued from the room which they usually occupied. The explanation is simple enough to us who know the real circumstances of the case. The cries and exclamations, and seeming conversation, were not all imaginary ; as will be seen in the fragment of Lady Arundel's journal that has been preserved, and which, with her letter already given, were long treasured up by the female relative to whom they were addressed, and subsequently, upon that relative's death, passed into the hands of the present writer. Her agony at times would find vent in words—would expend itself in bitter cries, wrung from her by a sense of loneliness and desertion, which threatened to deprive her of reason.

To turn her thoughts from preying on themselves, she would, she says, " commit to memory long passages of poetry, and make the solitary valley echo to her recitation." Hence, the exaggerated reports that prevailed of cries and shrieks to be heard in the neighbourhood of the cottage, breaking on the stillness of the night. Hence, the imputation of insanity which, even down to the present day, is not unfrequently hazarded. Who, indeed, can tell what may have been the effects of such seclusion —

14

with one almost a mute for her companion
—upon a highly-wrought, sensitive mind,
such as we know Lady Arundel's to have
been ? Who could answer for his own senses
in solitary confinement ?   The prisoner has
the chaplain, and others of his kind, to
exchange a few words with daily.

But in Lady Arundel's case, throughout
the period of what may be called her confinement—that is, down to the last stage of
it—it is perfectly certain that she never
exchanged a word with any one (Miss
Wilson can hardly be considered an exception), and scarcely did a human being's voice
ever fall upon her ear. Who, then, can
altogether reject the notion of occasional
mental derangement ? Who can say, absolutely, that this poor lady's misfortunes
did not sometimes get the better of her
reason, and induce her as a relief to
rush out into the cooling night air, and

vent her sorrow in mournful, incoherent exclamations ?

And, in her companion's case, it is not surprising that—to one unacquainted with the distressing privation she laboured under— the frequently mysterious movements of her hands, and the unnatural sounds, so painful to hear, which occasionally proceeded from her when she would make known her meaning otherwise than by signs, might well suggest the notion of something unearthly—something that had nothing in common with human hopes or fears, with human joys or sorrows. Especially might this be the case, when coupled with those fixed, stony-grey eyes of hers, always endeavouring, as it were, to read your meaning. It was a face not to be forgotten when once seen : that self-contained, immoveable expression, as if dead to every human passion.

As said before, we have merely fragments

of Lady Arundel's journal, kept during the period of her seclusion at St. Knighton's. They are written on detached pieces of paper without much order or method, and would seem, from expressions that occur here and there, to have been intended for her aunt's eye alone; or, perhaps, to serve as memorials of what she had gone through, to recur to in some imaginary future, fondly pictured to herself, but, alas! never to be realized—a future to be spent, she may have imagined, in the society of that loved aunt to whom her letter was addressed, when she could look back, as upon a vision of the night, upon that dark, secluded valley with its running stream and ever falling water.

Some of those entries are interesting, as constituting the few remaining records of a compulsory seclusion from the world which has few parallels. Mixed up with them, and written in the same disjointed form, are a few fragmentary prayers and meditations, evidently intended for the writer's eye alone; and which, out of deference to the wishes of her almost only surviving near relative, are here omitted. The first of these entries was plainly written two or three months after the arrival of the two ladies at St. Knighton's, and they are continued, though at long intervals, until almost to the close of the writer's captivity—the last entry, consisting of a few blotted lines, having been written before her final deliverance from the sorrows of life, and from the hard usage she had so long experienced at the hands of one who had vowed to "love and cherish her" unto his life's end!

"*Aug.* 3.—A day of gloom and sadness. It was on this very day three years I accepted Sir Edward's offer, to my sorrow, and forgot all R.'s past love and tenderness for me. Most justly have I been punished! Oh, how well do I recollect poor papa's look of satisfaction

all the evening, and how tenderly he kissed
me before going to bed! And here I am,
in this gloomy valley, hundreds and hundreds
of miles away from my father's house, and
from dearest Aunt Cary, whom I may never
see again!

"*Aug.* 10.—Such a sad dream! Dreamt
I was at home, and with R. by my side,
walking in the garden; he telling me all
his plans and hopes for the future, and saying
that his father was quite anxious to receive
me as his daughter-in-law! And then we
strolled out into the orchard, as we used to
do in those happy days, and sat down near
the river on a stump of a tree that had
been blown down; little Carlo was frisking
about, and he somehow got into the river,
and tried to clamber up the steep bank, but
wasn't able. And I dreamt that Reginald
got up and was pulling him out, when the
bank gave way, and there was a splash, and

I awoke in a fright. I listened for a moment, and couldn't think where I was; but soon the sound of the water-fall brought everything back to my sorrowful memory!— reminded me of perished hopes—of bye-gone happiness never to return—of friends whom I shall never, perhaps, look on again!

" *Sept.* (no date.)—Dearest Mary Wilson in low spirits to-day; and no wonder, for she seldom hears anything of her family; she would like to write and make inquiries, but she is afraid of giving Sir E. a handle to remove her from me altogether: and then she is sacrificing herself also, I know, for the benefit of her brothers and sisters, whom she is able to educate by remaining in this gloomy solitude. Oh, how much of good and self-denying kindness is there in her! and I do not think enough of it, and of all she is giving up for my sake, and that of her family. What a mystery is she to me, with that pale, anxious, inquiring face of hers—and I am, no doubt, to her ! When she sheds tears, there is something fearful about it ! She weeps so silently—doesn't sob, or moan, or anything of that sort. Well, if ever I am released from here, she shall experience my gratitude for all she has done for me.

" *Sept.* 21.—What a profusion of wild flowers all about this valley, and fern, and lichen, and heath, and mosses ! I have been all this fine morning arranging my collection of them, with Mary Wilson's assistance, and we have both been all the better for the occupation, I think. I have felt more hopeful, and she, poor thing, brightened up at times, so as quite to surprise me.

" *Oct.* 5.—I have been turning over plans of escape. There would be no difficulty about getting away; but where could I go ? who would receive me ? Papa gave me up

at once, when I fled to him for protection,
though I told him how cruelly Sir E. had
used me; and then I know how powerless
poor dear papa is, after all, to help me.
He told me himself on that miserable day
I drove to Bertram—or it was Mrs. B., I
think—how completely they were all at the
mercy of Sir Edward: really as much so as
ever; and that if papa were to take my part,
or receive me into his house, it would be
in Sir Edward's power to ruin him; which
he would not be slow in doing. Did not,
indeed, my husband tell me as much—
threaten me what he would do to papa—on
that day we had such a violent quarrel about
Mrs. Barry being in the house? Then, if
I was to go to dear Aunt Cary's, Sir Edward
could take me from her: and besides he
would visit papa with his displeasure all the
same.

" Where, then, can I go, if I leave this ?

Who will have me? Would Sir Edward have any scruples in locking me up in a lunatic asylum? How easily, with all his money and cleverness, to get persons to swear that I am mad, and doctors to sign away my liberty for life! Alas! I feel at times as if I *should* go mad. The desolation and silence of this place, only for that eternal water-fall, appals and frightens me. I fancy I see spirits moving about the valley in the dusk of the evening, and hear wailing voices and lamentations, and I long to add my own to them out of very bitterness of spirit! How gladly could I lie down and die in this sequestered spot, with the distant sound of the waves in my ears, far away from my own dear home, and from all whom I have loved there so well!"

Here there is a gap in the journal. Either no entries were made for the next few months, or the detached pieces of paper on which the journal was written have been lost or abstracted. At any rate no entry occurs again until

" *May* 17.—How pleasant and mild the air feels after the unusual severity of the winter—unusual, at least, I should think, in these western parts;—for what can the winters be here in comparison with the north? At my own dear home, this month is frequently as cold, almost, as any in the year. And then how the wild flowers abound in this beautiful valley!—for beautiful it would be in my eyes, but for being confined to it. Wild hyacinths, cowslips, primroses, fern, wood anemone—how they all abound, and how fragrantly smell! And then, the wild clematis—in what picturesque folds does it hang from the trees! how gracefully cluster about the porch! Ah, me! Even in this place one might be happy if one had one's liberty, and with a mind at ease! What have I not gone through in the winter, during the wet weather, when there was no stirring out—alone with poor Mary Wilson and my own dismal thoughts? I have felt, at times, as if I could not endure this sort of life much longer. I am sure my health is failing. Those spasms about my heart return oftener and oftener, and I fear that there is no cure for them! I have suffered from them more or less almost as long as I can recollect ; but they have lately increased in violence, and this damp situation must be bad for me. I have written once to Sir Edward since I have been here, but have had no answer. Well, I sometimes fear that I am fated never to quit this place : indeed, I have ceased to care much about living !

" Everything has seemed to go wrong with me since I broke faith with Reginald. Where is he now ? Can he have any idea of the place of my confinement? He would hardly leave me here if he knew of it. How I should like to see him again, if it was only once, just to ask his forgiveness—to be sure that he had quite forgiven me all the misery and wrong I have wrought him; and then, if it was God's will, to lie down and die—die in this sequestered valley, and be forgotten! for my life has been nothing but a burden to me for this ever so long, and I do not care how soon I part with it. My husband has cast me off, and I know his temper too well to suppose that he will ever relent or change his purpose; and there are those about him now who will take care that he never does, even if so inclined. He believes I have wronged him past forgiveness: imprudent I have certainly been, and so there is no help for me."

With this long extract closes Lady Arundel's diary, so far as it has been preserved.

CHAPTER XVI.

A CHAPTER UPON CHURCH MATTERS.

REGINALD TRELAWNEY's labours at Montacute did not appear to be crowned with any
remarkable share of success. The same
wayward, impulsive character, which has been
already remarked on as a peculiarity of the
Cornish peasantry, showed itself in everything. An eager curiosity, and overwhelm-
ing interest exhibited, followed almost directly by total indifference, and a turning to something else. It might be said of
most of them (when not at "*Bal*") that
"they spent their time in nothing else but

either to tell, or to hear some new thing;" or they might be compared to children with a new toy—all eagerness to examine it at first, but ready to throw it aside a few moments afterwards.

Was it lectures, or night-schools, or singing-classes that Trelawney tried?—the success would be most encouraging, the room crowded, an enlargement talked of. But the misfortune was that all this excitement lasted but for the first few times—it would subside quite as rapidly as it sprung up; and the whole herd—true to their Cornish motto, "one and all,"— would disappear *en masse*, much as they had arrived. No particular reason would be assigned, only that they had got tired of the thing, and wanted novelty. They are a gregarious race, are these Cornish miners. If one youth, tired of having been in the same place for so many minutes, and with having nothing to amuse him, gets up in the middle of service-time—and, with the most complete disregard as to what the parson or any one else may think of him, claps on his hat and walks out of church, making as much noise and clatter as he can—half-a-dozen other youths in different parts of the church, or who have been sitting all in a row together, looking over a sheet of " curls," it may be, and humming the tunes, are almost sure to start up and follow their companion's example, stamping out of church, and indulging in a good hearty laugh when just outside the door : it may be presumed, either at the parson's expense, who seemed so put out, or in order to assert their own free British independence. And it is well, if at intervals during the service, or the sermon, the same thing is not kept up—a perpetual going in and out of church.

Nor is this practice by any means con-

fined to the young men. They are fully
kept in countenance by the mine-girls,
who of the two possess a trifle more
of assurance. But what are their parents
and sober elders about? Unfortunately,
when a person takes a "serious turn" in
West Cornwall, he immediately thinks it
necessary to attend the meeting-house,
otherwise his pretensions to spirituality
would be pretty generally called in question.
No "converted" person, it is thought,
has any business in church: he will hear
nothing there that has any "savour of
doctrine" about it. No! the meeting-house
is the place for him; and, perhaps, he may
be prevailed on, nothing loth, to give a
minute account of his "conversion," or to
relate his "experience," for the edification of
those grave, sober-looking, rather severe coun-
tenanced individuals of both sexes, who regularly frequent the Bible-Christians' Chapel.

15

So the "young youths," and the "maids"
who work at the stamps, have it pretty
much all their own way in the spacious
half-empty church over the way—built with
a view rather to what might be hoped than
expected in the way of church-going amongst
the miners. The "serious" people are
all at the meeting-house, and the few elders
who do come to church are too often either
dependants upon the parson's charity, or
employed by him; or else persons whose
reputation for morality or sobriety has been
blown upon, and who favour church rather
than chapel principally from a notion that
there is less strictness required in one than
the other, and from a general distaste
to over-much religion, or any interference
with a man's private habits, be they what
they may.

Unfortunately it is the universal feeling
among the lower orders in Cornwall that

there is greater strictness observed, and
more extensive religious privileges to be
enjoyed, by chapel people than by church
people; and it is easily seen to what extent this is true. "What every one says
must be true," is a generally received
though most fallacious maxim; and as
long as it is the popular opinion among
the lower orders in Cornwall that Methodism and sanctity are convertible terms—as
much so as church and worldliness—the
mischief will keep increasing : the assertion
will be its own fulfilment. If a man wishes
to be thought serious, he considers it necessary to attend the meeting-house in preference to the church; and *that* quite irrespective
of his clergyman's merits or demerits.

Every clergyman in West Cornwall knows
what is the usual result of a "revival" in his
parish. His most promising Sunday school
children disappear from their class next Sun-

day: they have been "converted," and intimate their intention of going to chapel in
future.   And the same with any rather
promising young men or women, who may
have interested him.   They have perhaps
been prepared for Confirmation by him,
and they have hitherto passed scathe free
through Revivals; but their turn comes. So-
and-so has been " converted," "has been
taken-down," as they say, and their empty
place in church confirms the intelligence.

As to the immorality which results from
these Revivals, there can be no second
opinion amongst competent judges. Coupled
with prayer-meetings at night,—their ordinary accompaniment—no one thing has
contributed more than they have to the low
state of morals, and of feminine virtue, in
Cornwall. *Simple* Methodism has its use in
that country, and on the whole is not ill
adapted to the peculiar temperament of its

inhabitants.   Something more stirring—
something that appeals more to the senses—
that lays more hold on the imagination than
the church's ordinary service (well adapted
though it be for the educated and refined
classes), is what the Cornish miner requires.
And then service only once a week—with
possibly a school-room lecture—does not
satisfy his spiritual requirements. Would not
a shorter—more musical, and, if possible,
daily—service be best calculated to fix the
naturally unstable Cornish miner, and retain
him in the church's fold ?

All praise is due to that eminent man who
has so long filled the see of Exeter, and who
has done all that *one* man can possibly do
for his extensive diocese ; yet who can tell
the benefit that might accrue to Cornwall
and its inhabitants by the residence amongst
them of a bishop of their own, who would
apply his mind to adapt the church's minis-

trations to the habits of thought and idiosyncracies of the very peculiar people over whom he would be placed ?

Our readers must be pleased to attribute the foregoing reflections in substance to Tre-lawney, as the result of his labours at Montacute, and as accounting for the small measure of success which seemed to attend them.

CHAPTER XVII.

A CLERICAL DINNER PARTY.

As is the case in most country districts thinly inhabited by gentry, and where the clergy, who live necessarily at some distance apart from each other, make up the society, a spirit of hospitality is widely diffused in Cornwall. Where your nearest visiting neighbour lives some half-dozen miles off, and with an execrable road between you, there is little probability of your seeing very much of each other unless it be at the social board. Either you must tempt him, or he must tempt you, with a good dinner to make

it worth any one's while to brave the ele-
ments; which are frequently in a very
uproarious, uncomfortable state during the
dinner-giving season, that lasts some three
or four months, until all festivities are put a
stop to by grim Lent. When that season
is over, and winter has passed away with
a few parting hail-storms, then it is that
the Cornish parson begins to spread his
wings, and thinks it is time, after being
cooped up in such an outlandish place
for so many months, to take a flight somewhere, and see what is going on in London, or have a look at Paris, or climb the
Grands Mulets.

Accordingly, after the archdeacon's visitation, which takes place in May—and which
has the effect of gathering together, from
many a distant and sea-washed parsonage,
friends who, except upon such occasions,
never meet:—when this important event is

over, and the name has been duly answered to ; when the elaborate sermon (which has been a twelvemonth in. preparation, and is expected to produce *such* a sensation—only it doesn't,) has been decorously listened to, with fervent aspirations from high and low that it might shortly come to a close ; when the charge has been delivered—which is usually composed of a summary of the Acts of Parliament relating to the Church passed during the previous session, of some enlivening statistics about the " Religious Societies," of a few quiet hits at theological and political opponents of the Church, and an off-hand disposal of any doctrinal disputes which may have been disturbing the minds of the Church people since the period of the last visitation; then—after the dinner has been partaken of at the " Royal George," or the " King's Arms," or wherever it may be, and the standard toasts, " The Queen,"

" The Bishop," " The Preacher, with thanks, &c. &c., for his truly able and excellent sermon," " The Archdeacon," have been duly honoured—comes the general breaking up, and shaking of hands, until another twelvemonth comes round, and brings them together again from their remote parsonages.

After all this is over (*the* great event of the year to the clerical mind, unless it be the visitation of the Lord Bishop himself), and when the wives, and little olive-branches who have attained to years of discretion, have been summoned by Pater-familias out of the confectioner's shop, where they have been consuming their frugal meal of veal pies and buns; and after carriages and vehicles of all sorts have driven off—from the smart barouche with its pair of horses, and liveried servant, and which is occupied by the gaily-dressed wife and daughters of the rector of

St. Timothy, who is himself driving, down
to the little dingy rattle-trap of a phae-
ton in which the perpetual curate of St.
Mungo is "tooling" himself and his fat
wife out of town: after one and all these
events are over, then ensues a flight of
parsons—that is, of the rector of St.
Timothy stamp: men who can afford it—
eastward, not to see much of each other
until the return of winter brings with it the
usual round of festivities.   Then it is that
well-endowed rectors and vicars spread for
each other the ample board, and gladly summon to the feast, any "well-conditioned"
clerical stranger in the neighbourhood,
who may haply have alighted on Cornish
soil.

Under this head Trelawney was unani-
mously pronounced to come, and so his invitations to "good men's feasts" during the
season were unintermitting.   There was a

trifle of sameness, it must be allowed, amongst the guests; for, except in the case of a stranger like himself, Trelawney usually met the same people over and over again. Those who didn't entertain were socially extinct : no one seemed to know anything about them—hadn't seen them for ever so long, though living in the adjoining parish; so that etiquette and good taste forbade any mention of such people : there were much pleasanter subjects to talk about. ·

Let us listen to the conversation upon one of these festive occasions :—What is the rector of St. Timothy, that tall, gentle- manly, middle-aged looking man, who looks so well preserved, and so young to be the father of grown-up daughters,— what is he talking about to the young Rector of St. Julian, whose arrival in the neighbourhood, with his pretty highly-born wife, has been pronounced *such* an acquisition? Why, what should those two be talking about but their Cochin-China-fowl?—in praises of which they are quite enthusiastic. Then they get to the subject of the best breed of pigs, and modes of fattening them. So that you see clerical and theological subjects did not by any means engross the after dinner conversation; but politics, agriculture, mining affairs, all in their turn came under review. For is not the vicar of St. Crispin the best authority in the county on the subject of mines—which are " safe," which " shaky? "—and could he not give you a wrinkle or two as to the best mine in which to take shares? So that the words, " consols," " sets," " lodes," " grass" and " mine captains," came to be pretty well mixed up with such expressions as " such spurs," " such a comb," " such a crow as it has," or, " splendid boar," " beautiful little porker," "short hair," "good grain," &c.

Thus some such cross-conversation as this would go on,—

"I have it on Captain Dick's own authority;" "but then you should see my bird's tail, and legs, they *are* beauties:" "why the water is coming in so fast that I expect shares will be below par as soon as ever the adventurers come to —— :" "I like to hear it crow myself, and then its eggs—some people object:" "Depend upon it, that Captain Michael Oats knows what he is about; why he told me himself in confidence that he and Mr. Gully—— :" "I expect her to litter next month, and you shall have one of them if you like:" "and so that is the way, Captain Dick says, those people in London got so fearfully let in:" &c.

Much of this was not of a nature to interest a stranger; however, there were not wanting those who were disposed for something more general. Accordingly some such conversation as this would be started :—

"Well, how do you like Cornwall, Mr. Trelawney, and where you are?"

"I shall be able to answer you better after a time, when I get more acquainted with the place and people."

"You will never be able to make anything of them; they are all Dissenters in these parts."

"Well, I mean to try, by having short services of an evening, and lectures."

"All that has been tried by me at St. Bridget's, but to no purpose. I now go on the plan of being very strict with them,—requiring forty-eight hours' notice before I perform any funerals, and I take no one into church who hasn't been in the habit of attending regularly."

"How do they like that, Marsh?" asked the vicar of St. Lawrence, "for I have thoughts of doing it too."

"They don't seem to like it at all, but I am determined to reduce them to obedience."

"You two men, Marsh and Thresham, mustn't think to do anything by driving your people; you must try and lead them. If you were Cornishmen you would know that," observed Mr. Polcarn, a mild-eyed, quiet, useless little man, who had scarcely ever been out of the county since his college days.

"Well, Polcarn, it seems to me to come to pretty much the same thing whether you lead them or drive them; they seem fully determined to have their own way."

"How is your church attended?" asked Trelawney of Mr. Marsh.

"Very few come now, I am happy to

say.   You look surprised; but I am sick
of humouring these Methodists, and I let
them know that I only want to have good
sound Churchmen about me, and so I have
weeded my congregation most effectually;
and now, though only a few come, yet it
is a comfort to know that they are all sound
church people."

"I never," observed meek little Mr.
Polcarn, who seemed anxious to say something, and who plainly considered that, on
the strength of his being a Cornishman, he
alone knew how his countrymen ought to
be "managed;" "I never, for my part,
interfere with them in any way whatever,
where their own peculiar customs are
concerned, but take it all very quietly,
and this I find to be the best plan 'after
all.'"

"No doubt it is the easiest and quietest,"
said Trelawney, with a smile at the little

man's self-complacency ; " but what do you mean by not interfering with them ? "

" Why, Marsh there objects, I know, to their habit of crowding into church at funerals and weddings, and keeping their hats on there, and seizing on the bells, and ringing them, and going out of church during service time, and those sort of things."

" Well, and your plan ? "

" My plan is not to make or meddle with them. They would never give me any peace if I did. They would do to me what they used to do to my predecessor, I am told."

" What was that ?"

" Why, wait for him until he came out of church, and then form an avenue, and oblige him to walk through their ranks for some distance, they all the time singing Methodist hymns (which they knew he hated) at the very top of their voices, and finishing up with a loud laugh before they would let

him go. And they did the same very often
when he went out for a walk, and happened
to fall in with them.   He was a nervous
man, was poor Fraser—he is dead now—and
so he used, I am told, to jump over the hedge
whenever he saw any of these young men
standing in the road together, in order to
avoid them.   They used to give him no end
of trouble ; at last he was glad to exchange
livings with me, and he went eastward to
St. Uney, and there died.   He got all this
ill-will because he tried to stop the Methodist
hymn they are so fond of singing at funerals.
So I say the best plan is to leave them
alone."

"How is your church attended ?" asked
Trelawney : " well, I hope, as the result of
all this conciliation."

" I can't say it is.   Indeed, with the exception of Sir Roger Pendragon and his
family and servants, and my own family,

very few attend : but I have ceased to trouble myself about it."

" Each leaves the other alone ? "

" Exactly."

" And that is the best plan you can devise with all your experience ?"

" It is."

The little man refreshed himself with another glass of sherry, and then joined in the general move into the next room.

CHAPTER XVIII.

MRS. TRESSILIAN GIVES HER OPINION.

" WELL, but you must allow, my dear, that he *is* peculiar—that he has got some odd ways about him. He looks so strange and startled at times."

These and similar remarks Mrs. Tressilian was pouring into her husband's reluctant ears one morning after breakfast, as they were alone in the latter's study. Now Mr. Tressilian was particularly busy at that very time upon his celebrated work on zoophytes (noticed so favourably in a *Journal of Philosophical Transactions*, published by the Cornish Literary Society), and, if the truth must be told, was very desirous to have his little room to himself; so that his answers were rather vague, and by no means came up to his wife's notions of the exigencies of the case. He was, besides (like many other men), much more taken up in studying the habits and peculiarities of birds and animals about him than in noticing what was passing in his own family and under his eyes. His wife—a plump, busy, active little body —was, he thought, quite capable of taking care of the concerns of the family, without appealing to him. When, therefore, she pressed him so perseveringly for his opinion about Trelawney, the worthy man was somewhat at a loss what to say.

" Well, my love, I don't know that I ever remarked anything particular about him, or unlike other people. I know we get on very well together. He has got some odd notions

about poetry, if that's what you mean : he
admires Spenser, and Chaucer, and the early
English writers, while, as you know, I'm a
devout Miltonian."

" My dear Charles, I am not likely to
trouble myself about his poetical fancies.
No, what I say is that he evidently admires
our Charlotte, and if you were anybody else
you would take notice of it."

" How does he show it ? Has he said
anything to her ?"

" No ; that is the puzzle. But I am not
blind, my dear ; and if you were not so taken
up with those stupid creatures that you are
writing about all day long, you would see
things as I do."

" Well, what do you want me to do
exactly ?" asked Mr. Tressilian, making a
great display of settling himself to go on
with his writing, and dipping his pen in the
ink. " If you will only tell me what I am

expected to do, and then leave me in peace to go on with my writing. I have come to the most important part of my treatise— about the organs of respiration, and really I shall get confused if I am not left alone."

" How tiresome you are! and all about those miserable little wretches, or whatever they are. I want you to be like other fathers, and to talk about our girls, and to see what is for their advantage. Whenever I speak to you at night you are so sleepy that I am sure you are not paying any attention."

" Very possibly. Well, come, what is it?" and the rector put down his pen in despair.

" Oh, I think that we ought to make some inquiries about Mr. Trelawney's previous history. He is on a very intimate footing in our family, and I can't help thinking has some views with respect to Charlotte?"

" Well, what if he has ? He is of a very respectable family, we know that. I *just* remember his father living in this county. They took the name of Trelawney, you know, upon coming in for some property in the north ; or this young man's grandfather did, at any rate, and the family have not resided in Cornwall for ever so long."

" It is not so much about his family I want to speak, for that is all right enough ; or about his property, for I have heard him allude casually to some family living in the north that is to be his some day or other. It is not about these I am uneasy ; but I should like to know something about his own previous history. There always seems to me to be an air of mystery about him. He is so reserved ; he seldom speaks about himself. Do you know, I sometimes think he may be already married,—or engaged perhaps. There is something I am sure on his mind, and which prevents him from proposing for Charlotte."

" Why, you women are all such match-makers ! You are always fancying that people are in love, or going to propose, or something of that sort."

" Well, perhaps we are ; but you will admit that women are much more keen-sighted than you men."

" I readily admit it,—too keen-sighted, · by far, for you see things that have no existence except in your own imagination."

"However, we will not talk about that now, as I perceive you are longing to get back to your dear little zoophytes. Only I would have you keep your eyes open, and instead of having long conversations with him about poetry and nonsense of that sort, try and make out from him something of his own early history. It may lead him to say something; for it is never an advantage to a girl to have her name coupled with a young man's, as Charlotte's is with his, I know, unless something is likely to come of it."

"Well, I am a bad hand at trying to fish anything out of a person. But perhaps he may say something of himself that might give the conversation a turn in the direction you wish."

"Well, I wouldn't lose any time about it. Ask him to dine, and talk about Northumberland; that is what I should do."

"I wish you would, then; you would do it much better than I should. However, we can't ask him to dine at present, for he has gone from home for the week."

"Men *are* such cowards. But where is he gone to? You can speak to him when he comes back."

"Well, we'll see about it. He has gone upon an excursion up the north coast as far as Tintagel. He has never seen the place, he told me. I don't suppose he will be back for a few days."

"Well, there is nothing to be done about it at present, I see."

"Nothing," echoed her husband, in a tone of great satisfaction. "And now for my essay."

In the meantime the unconscious subject of Mrs. Tressilian's strictures was carrying out a project upon which he had long set his mind—a pedestrian tour along the north coast. For any one suffering from depression of spirits, or over anxiety, there is no remedy like a tour on foot through interesting scenery; especially if that scenery lies, as in this instance it did, along the coast.

The north coast of Cornwall is pre-eminent for its wild savage grandeur, for its precipitous cliffs, and for the ceaseless thundering noise of the waves which are dashed up against it in mighty billows. On other sides of the Cornish coast the sea is frequently calm, but here on the north coast it never is; for, owing to a continual ground-swell, the sea rolls in with terrific grandeur, and breaks upon the rocks with a voice of thunder. You have nature here in all its majesty; and, whether you are alone, or with another, the spectacle is alike well calculated to take you out of yourself—to still all mere human passions; to fill you with unspeakable awe and reverence. And it was not long before Trelawney experienced the sedative effects derivable from a contemplation of such glorious works of nature.

To him Isabella Arundel was now as one dead,—so long was it since he had seen her, or had any sure tidings of her fate. That fate was wrapped up in mystery; though the opinion gradually gained ground that she had been placed in a convent

abroad. Her husband was travelling in the
East, and, having relinquished the active
part he had formerly taken in the management of his bank, it was thought probable
that his stay abroad would be a lengthened
one. Any communication now with Isabella
seemed to Trelawney hopeless, and hardly
to be desired even if it were possible.

What were the thoughts rising in her
former lover's mind only a twelvemonth ago ?
—when he stood upon that lonely hill of
Montacute, and saw all nature in sweet
repose about him—all seemingly happy, because pursuing their peaceful callings, and
" dwelling amongst their own people." And
then when he reflected upon himself—driven
in a manner from his own home and belongings—baulked of his long-expected inheritance—robbed most nefariously of his affianced
bride—what were the wild, stormy thoughts
which once had had possession of him ?

Why, to throw up an uncongenial employment, to walk over Europe, if need be, in
search of his early and first love, to tear
her from her tyrant's grasp, and carry her
triumphant to distant lands.

But better thoughts than these had been
since gaining the ascendancy over him—
thoughts of God and holiness—thoughts of
purity and self-denial—thoughts of submission to the divine will, and of devotion to
that work to which he had " set his hand."
The soothing effects of his intercourse with
the Tressilian family, and a participation in
their quiet home pursuits and innocent recre-
ations, had begun to tell upon his embittered
spirit; to turn his thoughts away from his
own misery and disappointments ; to make
him long for the quiet happiness of home and
a domestic life. Such a holy calming influence may the spectacle of a bright, happy,
refined family circle exercise over the most

distempered mind—over the most seemingly
blighted affections! And then as for the
girls, where in all Cornwall were there any
prettier, more lively, good, useful, cheerful-
tempered girls than were Charlotte and
Loveday Tressilian? And if Trelawney did
not throw himself at the feet of one of
them, and beseech her to accept him—as
their fond careful mamma seemed to think
he ought—we may suppose it was more
from an unwillingness to sever the last tie
which seemed still to bind him to Isabella—
the fond, often-dwelt-upon recollection of
what they had been to each other—than
any insensibility to the charms of Charlotte
Tressilian, or indifference to be thought
worthy of such a treasure.

Such thoughts as these coursed through
and through the tourist's mind, as, leaving
behind him the *towans* of Hayle, Trelawney
turned his face towards St. Agnes and

Perranzabuloe, and allotted himself three days to explore all the wild interesting scenery which lay between him and the far-famed castle of Tintagel—the birthplace of King Arthur, and scene of so many of his achievements.

CHAPTER XIX.

THE "VALLEY OF THE MILL."

WE do not propose accompanying Trelawney very closely in his tour along the north coast. We shall not, therefore, stay to narrate how he ascended St. Agnes' lofty beacon, or explored the sandy dunes of Perranzabuloe — an immense waste, with countless rabbits as the only denizens, and the *arundo arenaria* the only vegetation ; where clouds of sand, in perpetual motion, darken the horizon; where, after wandering by the hour amidst a scene of appalling desolation, the traveller may chance to light upon an old four-holed cross in the midst of the desert, and stumble upon some scattered ruins : once a church—and buried for a thousand years beneath the sand. We need not dwell upon these things. Are they not written in John Murray his book ? Nor shall we be tempted—though great the temptation—to turn aside with Trelawney, and rest a while in Lanherne's pleasant vale, with its grey convent of Carmelite nuns ; once the manor-house of the " great Arundels," and whose cloistered inmates are never visible to mortal eye : a vale where, despite the few scattered cottages, an almost unbroken silence ever prevails, save from the murmuring of the little stream, which courses along ; and where wide-spreading trees and steep banks covered with moss and fern, all contribute to the air of perfect repose which here reigns supreme.

We pass on with unwilling steps to where Trelawney's fate is conducting him,

" not knowing," and where all the secret, mysterious influences which have been so long drawing him, are converging, before being dissipated for ever.

It was on a bright, sunshiny morning, then, that Reginald Trelawney at length stood beneath the grey dismantled walls of Tintagel — the " dark Dundagil by the Cornish sea ; " the scene of so many romantic tales. There King Arthur reigned, and Sir Launcelot of the Lake, and Sir Galahad, and Sir Tristram, and others of the " Knighthood-errant of the Realm," were drawn in that fair order of the Table Round—

" A glorious company, the flower of men,"

who were

> " To ride abroad redressing human wrongs ;
> To speak no slander ; no, nor listen to it ;
> To lead sweet lives in purest chastity ;
> To love one maiden only, cleave to her,
> And worship her by years of noble deeds,
> Until they won her."

Some hours had elapsed before Trelawney could quit a place fraught with so many stirring recollections of the past; whose ruins,—now almost surrounded by the waves, and against whose foundation-stones the billows of the sea are ever breaking with tumultuous violence—had in the days of their pristine glory beheld so many knightly warriors and fair dames, the fair and beauteous Guinevere at their head, gathered within their walls. Time sped swiftly by while wrapt up in such thoughts, and the shadows were beginning to lengthen before Trelawney could fairly turn his back upon the castle, and begin to descend from the lonely heights upon which it stands. His face was now to be directed homeward. He had reached the extreme point of his tour, as arranged before quitting Montacute; the week, too, was drawing to a close, and the Sunday's duties to be thought of.

It was before the days of John Murray
and his red books ; but Itineraries, and
books of roads, with their bald description
of places, and names of inns, and lists of
gentlemen's seats, and accurate accounts of
mileage, supplied their place. In one of
these interesting Itineraries, which Trelawney had chanced to take up at the little
wayside inn where he had slept on the
previous night, he had read, under the head
of Tintagel : " Within a short distance to
the east is the valley of St. Knighton's,
remarkable for its waterfall. The cascade
falls a distance of thirty feet and seven
inches. There are several rare ferns and
mosses to be found here, amongst the rest
the *asplenum varigosa,* a great rarity, as
also the *cladophora Brownii.*

" Come, I'll go and see this waterfall,"
thought Trelawney to himself. " It will
just fill out the day; and I may be able

to pick up a fern or two, or some of
this moss, for Charlotte Tressilian."

A short walk brought him to the entrance of a valley with high hills on either
side. The foliage was more than usually
profuse, and mosses, and ferns, and trail-
ing plants which love the shade, abounded.
Trelawney had not advanced far up the valley when he felt the persuasion that the
place was familiar to him. He must have
visited it when a child, he thought, though
he had forgotten all about it; or perhaps
he had seen a picture of it somewhere.
"How strange!—and there's that mill—all
looking so picturesque about it, — why,
surely I have seen it before! It seems
all so perfectly familiar to me—this running stream and all — and the branches
dipping in the water—and then these steep
banks with all this fern. It reminds one
of what people say—that we have often a

consciousness of a previous state of existence; for it certainly seems as if I had
been here before."

The path which Trelawney was pursuing
was getting more and more entangled, and
he almost despaired of ever reaching the
waterfall; the noise of which, however,
was heard distinctly enough. At length
he reached a place where the hand of
man was visible, where a tolerable foot-
path was formed, and where the brambles
and underwood had been kept in something
like order. The silence, save for the
splashing sound of the waterfall, was complete—hardly even broken by the occasional twittering of a bird. An air of
perfect stillness pervaded the place, and
the arching trees overhead, with the declining daylight, all contributed to the prevailing gloom. It was not until Trelawney
had caught sight of the waterfall—the

water falling first into a sort of basin (Cornicè, Keive), and then tumbling down several feet into a lower level, and so finding its way down the valley—it was not until his eyes rested upon the waterfall that the truth rushed into his mind.

"My dream! my dream!" he cried out. "This is what I dreamt of at Cholmondeley: it was there I saw it all—this dark valley—these high hills shutting it in—this stream dancing and gurgling at my feet, and all about. I remember it now distinctly. Oh! can it be here—to this lonely place—they have brought my poor Isabel? She may not be abroad after all; but here, in this very valley—in this remote corner of England! Oh! what a heart could that man have to choose such a solitude for her!"

As Trelawney, in a whirl of excitement, was uttering these passionate exclamations

out loud, while leaning against a large ash-
tree which then stood a few yards to the
right of the cascade, and which partly concealed him, he was startled by perceiving,
standing within a few yards of him, the
identical figure in black which he had
seen in his dream. She was not, indeed,
wringing her hands, as then he beheld
her, but was perfectly still and motionless,
and gazing intently on the stream. There
was just the same stony look of despair
about her face that he remembered, only
she appeared older, and, if possible, more
sad.

Though Trelawney's emotion had led
him to utter wild, passionate exclamations
of grief, yet no impression was seemingly
made by them upon this sad lady: she
plainly did not hear them. Then all
at once it rushed upon Trelawney's mind
who Isabella's companion was: it must

be Mr. Wilson's deaf and dumb daughter; as he remembered to have been told all about it some time back, though it had almost escaped his recollection until now. It could, then, no longer admit of doubt that he beheld Isabella's companion in that sad, silent woman, who stood almost beside him.

Checking his first impulse to come forth from his place of concealment, Trelawney watched her motions; when, after pausing by the side of the stream for a few minutes, lost in thought as it would seem, the lady pursued her path, passing close by her observer, and took her way up a narrow path to the top of the bank. There stood a lonely cottage which Trelawney had not observed before; passing through the open door of it she disappeared. For some minutes Trelawney stood irresolute, whether to advance boldly to the house and claim

Isabella's liberty in the name of her father, or to wait his opportunity.

What if Miss Wilson should deny his right to interfere ? Was not Isabella still legally under the authority and protection of her husband ? and might it not aggravate the miseries of her confinement if a former lover were to step forward and claim an interest in her ? Nay, who could tell but that Miss Wilson had both the will and the power to enforce Isabella's submission to her authority ? Was it quite certain that the unhappy captive might not prefer residence even in such a place, and with such a companion, yet with still some degree of liberty, to being immured once more at Northington with hateful insults as her daily portion ?

Trelawney was balancing in his mind these doubts—at one time resolved, come what might of it, to demand to see Isabella,

and then to act according to circumstances—
but a moment afterwards arresting his steps
by the dread of increasing rather than
diminishing her sufferings, if he were to
do anything rashly—of perhaps hopelessly
riveting her chains instead of loosening
them.

While filled with these thoughts, from the
same door which Miss Wilson had entered,
issued another figure which, though ob-
scured by the failing light, Trelawney recognized instinctively as none other than Lady
Arundel. Oh, how his heart bounded within
him at the sight! What wild tumultuous
thoughts coursed through his mind as he
beheld his own beloved Isabella—his own
affianced wife that was, his all and all—as
he beheld her, after a turn or two in front
of the cottage, slowly approaching the
waterfall, and preparing to descend by the
little path which conducts into the valley!

Now was the time for disclosing himself. Trelawney waited until he could do so without the chance of being observed from the windows of the cottage.

Isabella approached his place of concealment; there was still some light, and when she threw back her veil, he saw that all her colour and animation were departed. It needed not that languid step of hers to proclaim that her health was suffering, that her captivity was telling upon her. Her pale face and sunken eyes told the truth plainly enough. She looked years and years older since Trelawney had last seen her. She descended the bank by the little foot-path, and passed near where Trelawney was. Slowly then she pursued her way down the valley, until coming to a rustic seat, she sat herself down with apparent listlessness, and seemed absorbed in thought—or in prayer, for her eyes were closed. When she opened them, her former lover was standing by her side.

" Oh, Isabella, my love, is it here I find you ? Yet, thank God, I have found you, and before it is too late. How is it you look so pale and thin ? I will never leave you until I take you out of this place and restore you to your family."

For a few moments Isabella was speechless with astonishment; and when words came to her relief, she spoke in feeble, faltering tones, very unlike her former clear, animated voice.

" Oh, Reginald, what can have brought you here ? has it been to seek me out ? Who has sent you ? The time was, and that not so long ago, only this time last year, that I could have welcomed you— welcomed almost any one, as a deliverer. But it is now too late. Something tells me that my course is nearly run—that I am

to end my days in this lonely valley: and
better that it should be so. My life has
not been so happy a one that I can wish
to have it prolonged. I have brought
nothing but trouble and sorrow upon those
belonging to me, by my own levity and
breach of faith towards you. I have been
to blame, as well as my husband. I should
have studied his temper, and been more
careful not to have given him any cause
of jealousy. God forgive those who have
set him against me, and who have told him
that about me—for their own ends, as I now
know—which might excuse him for hating
me, and putting me from him. But it was
all false. I had done nothing for which I
should have been imprisoned as I was at
Northington, or banished to this remote
place."

Isabella was deeply affected as she
uttered these words: her voice was fre-

quently broken by hysterical sobs. Trelawney judged it better, considering her state
of weakness, rather to strive and tranquillize
her than to agitate her by a recurrence to
the past.

"Dearest Isabel, you are not strong; and
it is late for you to be out; the mists are
rising in the valley. Let me meet you here
to-morrow at mid-day, and we shall be better
able than we are now to decide upon what
is to be done."

Soothing her with many kind words,
but inwardly much disturbed and alarmed
himself at the state of utter prostration in
which he had found the once lively and
high-spirited Isabella Bertram, Trelawney
conducted her towards the cottage. The
surprise and consequent agitation had been
too much for her weak frame. She made
an attempt or two to talk of old times,
but had to relinquish so painful an

18

effort; and leaning heavily on her former lover, she was conducted by him to within a few yards of the door of the cottage. Here they parted, but with the understanding that they should meet the next day.

CHAPTER XX.

" DEATH, THE CONSOLER."

ON the next day, Trelawney had not long
to wait for Isabel. She slowly approached
him, coming from the cottage; and, if he
had serious misgivings on the previous
evening as to her state of health, the daylight only served to confirm his unfavour-
able impressions. Her features were shrunk,
and her eyes looked unnaturally large. Her
voice, too, was altered, and the least fatigue
seemed too much for her.

" I have been thinking, Reginald, over
the past, and of what you said last night

18—2

about taking me away. I should like certainly to see papa again, and, if it were
God's will, to close my eyes at Bertram.
But I cannot leave here without the permission of either papa or my husband. If
they knew how ill I am, and have been
for some time past—though I have concealed it from Miss Wilson as well as I
could—they would not be for leaving me
here any longer. I want to see home and
friends once more—and then, God's will be
done! Do you let them know at home
where I am, and that I feel as if I had
not long to live: the rest I leave in God's
hands."

There was a tone of the deepest dejection
and hopelessness about Isabella's manner,
and in every word that fell from her, which
alarmed Trelawney more than he cared to
own. He could not but allow to himself
that, situated as Isabella was, with a jealous

and tyrannical husband, and with his spies possibly in the neighbourhood—and considering all the unfortunate consequences that had resulted from the last stolen interview between himself and the object of his former love — the utmost circumspection and prudence was required on both their parts to shield Isabella's fair fame from reproach.

Trelawney's own passions were now allayed. Time and reflection, and serious thoughts on the past, had effected this for him. And, as for poor Isabella herself, it was plain she had well nigh done with earthly passions, whether of love or hate; she herself was now no object to excite either. If she could be brought home to die, it was as much as could be expected.

Exacting, therefore, a promise that in the event of her health becoming worse, she would at once have recourse to the aid of the nearest medical man, Trelawney quitted her; with a sore heart, indeed, and with many pangs and misgivings. He had to hasten back to Montacute for the next day's duty; and on Monday he would proceed to the north without delay, in order to see Mr. Bertram, and arrange with him for Isabella's return home. They took a last tender farewell of each other, and then parted—for ever!

Monday saw Trelawney speeding his way northward. There were no railways in those days; but, as fast as four-horsed coaches could take him, he proceeded on his journey. Still the journey was then one of several days, go about it how you liked, from the extreme west to the extreme north of England; and it was past the middle of the week before Trelawney found himself driving up the approach to Bertram Hall. He was the bearer of important intelligence, besides that which related to Isabella. For in passing through Newcastle, and while changing horses, he had taken up the previous evening's London paper just arrived, and the following paragraph instantly arrested his attention under the head of " Constantinople.—(From our own correspondent). Sir Edward Arundel died here on the 18th, of cholera."

It was necessary to break the intelligence, with which Trelawney was fraught, somewhat carefully to Mr. Bertram, whose health was broken, and his temper rendered extremely irritable, by repeated attacks of gout. Under the circumstances, another messenger than Trelawney would have been preferable; for he was ostensibly the cause (so, at least, Mr. Bertram chose to believe) of all Sir Edward's cruelty towards his wife.

It was some time before the father could quite understand, or be induced, indeed, per-

fectly to credit, the circumstances under
which Trelawney had accidentally become
acquainted with the place of his daughter's
concealment. There was, besides, an uneasy
feeling of self-reproach on the part of Mr.
Bertram, that Isabella had been made a sacrifice on account of his own pecuniary difficulties. He felt that but for them, and the
unfair means resorted to by Mrs. Bertram to
break off her daughter's engagement, she
would long since have been the happy wife of
Reginald Trelawney. Altogether, some little
delay and difficulty intervened before Mr.
Bertram could be induced thoroughly to
bestir himself.

At length, and now that all real difficulties
were at an end, owing to Sir Edward's death,
Trelawney took his departure, armed with Mr.
Bertram's authority that his daughter should
be at once released from her banishment and
sent home. It was at first intended that

Mr. Bertram should accompany Trelawney on this welcome errand; but failing health forbade him. So, requesting Trelawney to make arrangements for the reception of his daughter and her companion at the house of a female relative of Isabella's, who lived at Exeter, he saw his guest depart westward a few days after his arrival at Bertram Hall.

As may be imagined, Trelawney seemed to fly on his errand; and travelling day and night whenever it was possible, he finally found himself alighting from the Exeter coach, in the street of Carnelford, exactly on the tenth day since his departure to the north. He was soon on the road to St. Knighton's, being driven in some nondescript vehicle from the hotel. The driver was not particularly communicative, nor was Trelawney in any mood for conversation; so they pursued the drive in silence.

In the distance he saw the gray, pin-
nacled tower of the parish church of St.
Knighton's; presently, a dull, heavy sound,
as of a bell, fell on his ear—and then
another stroke after a time—and another.
In certain frames of mind, and especially
after an absence, long or short, the mind is
peculiarly sensitive of impressions. Trelawney feared to ask any questions of the
driver: he dreaded the answer. As they
approached the churchyard, a funeral pro-
cession was seen issuing from the church;
the white surpliced minister appeared, followed by the coffin and its bearers.

" Whose funeral would it be ?" at last
Trelawney summoned up courage to inquire
of the driver.

" Don't know rightly, sir," he answered
carelessly—" one of the ladies of the cottage, it may be—I hear one of them is
gone dead."

"Which of them, for God's sake?" cried Trelawney, grasping his arm.

"Can't say, sir—will ask this man. I say, my son, whose funeral be it?"

"One of the ladies of the cottage," the man said, indifferently.

"Which of them?"

"Don't know their names, sir,—nobody does. But it is the younger of the two, I heard our folks say."

A mist passed across Trelawney's eyes. He stopped the horse, and got out of the carriage, hardly knowing what he did. He made his way through the crowd which surrounded the churchyard. He approached the grave side.

"We give Thee hearty thanks for that it hath pleased Thee to deliver this our sister out of the miseries of this mortal life," said the clergyman, solemnly.

"Oh, God! oh, God! it is true, then,—

it is all true,—and I have come too late.
Dear, dear beloved Isabella, and have you
died after all in your prison house; and has
freedom come to you too late! Dear, dear
love, would to God I could have died for
you!"

Trelawney had turned aside in bitter
anguish as he uttered these words.

The crowd was dispersing, and the
clergyman—a middle-aged, matter-of-fact
looking man—after a slight glance of pro-
fessional curiosity at the stranger, took his
departure. Trelawney looked into the open
grave. There was no plate on the coffin.
The sexton gave him what information he
could.

"We heard tell on Saturday, sir, that
one of the ladies was dead. She was found
dead in her bed, sir, I believe. The
doctor said it was heart complaint, and
that it had been coming on some time.

So my wife and some of the neighbours went up there, and had her laid out, and tried to comfort the other poor lady, and to take her away. But she wouldn't come. She wept a deal, they say, but couldn't be got to utter a word. And some do say that she be deaf and dumb like. But Captain Will—he who owns the cottage— says he thinks the lady is possessed of a spirit: she is not altogether like one of us. She do shed tears in an odd fashion, he says; that is, she makes no noise: doesn't sob, or moan, or cry out like other people."

"And this is all that is known of the other poor lady's death?" asked Trelawney, endeavouring to restrain his emotion so as not to attract the sexton's notice, who was busy shovelling in the earth over all that remained of the lovely and high-spirited Isabella Bertram.

"This is all that is known of her death,

sir. They lived very retired, them two ladies did, in the cottage in the valley, and all kinds of tales were told of them— as how they lived on slugs, and things of that sort. No one knows their names; and parson was saying just now that he was at a fine loss what to put in the register about her. They kept her as long as possible in hopes of some of her friends turning up to claim her."

"And how is the other poor lady?"

"I haven't seen her myself this brave bit, but my missus has been up there two or three times since the death of the other one, and has tried to get her to eat summat, but she can prevail nothing. And so Captain Will talks of going over to Lawyer Pearce in Wadebridge, to ask him what is to be done."

It was now dusk and too late for anything to be done that evening; so Trelawney,

with a heavy heart and blighted hopes, went
to the inn where he had previously stopped,
determining to seek out the lonely occupant
of the cottage in the morning.

CHAPTER XXI.

CONCLUSION.

But "man proposes, God disposes." The
fatigue and excitement of the last ten days,
coupled with the mental anguish endured on
finding that death had forestalled him, and
opened the doors of the prison-house without
his intervention, proved too much for Trelawney's strength. In the morning he was
in a high fever. Racking, shooting pains,
accompanied with shiverings and burning
heat, and soon succeeded by delirium, left
no doubt that Trelawney was dangerously
ill; and so quickly did the fever gain on him

that he became soon perfectly unconscious of all that was going on about him. For days and days did he toss about on that sick bed in the little inn—his thoughts turning almost entirely on home and early days. The name of Isabella was perpetually on his lips : sometimes he upbraided her, sometimes fondly called upon her; sometimes it was as if he endeavoured to save her from some great danger—sad, plaintive words did they seem to the attendants in the sick room. Then his thoughts would seem to fly off at once to the gloomy valley of St. Knighton's, and he would shudder, and cry out, and moan most piteously. Still, no one who heard his broken words thought of connecting the two together—the poor lady he was so constantly raving about, and the valley of St. Knighton, which it was supposed he must have lately visited, from his frequent allusions to it.

"He got a chill there may be—staying out too late—and so he got the fever." This was nurse's explanation. She was too much accustomed to her business to attach much importance to the ravings of any one in a fever. And so, for many a day, with Trelawney it was a battle for life or death : the village doctor came and went, and shook his head and gave ambiguous answers, and every morning it was expected that the church bell would denote the passing of another soul into eternity. The simple villagers would inquire of the landlady of the little inn as they passed, how the sick gentleman was going on ; and for days together the answer would be the same—"No better —the doctor thinks he can't hold out much longer." But at length it began to be whispered that the sick gentleman was likely to get over it, after all. "With great care," the doctor had said, "he might pull through it ;"

and then, through gradual steps of convalescence, with occasional relapses, Trelawney began to regain his strength—was able to thank his doctor, and finally was pronounced, " all right again."

It was during these first stages of recovery, and from the lips of the bustling, good-tempered landlady, that Trelawney was put in possession of what had occurred during his illness.

" We did all we could, sir, to comfort the other poor lady that was at the cottage, after the death of the first one ; and I brought her up myself a sup of broth and a pudding, to see if she could be got to take anything ; but all to no purpose. She wished to be ' left alone,' so she wrote upon a piece of paper. And so, finding it was all in vain, I came away ; but some of the neighbours went up to the cottage every day. They didn't like to go in—being timorous like—and especially

after what Captain Will had said—that she
was possessed of an evil spirit, which prevented her speaking. But they looked in
at the window, and there they always saw
the poor lady sitting in the one seat which
she had always occupied. And so this went
on for ten days or a fortnight; at last
one of Hanibal Polkinghorne's little maids
going up there—she is a forward, daring
little thing, and always was—and, looking
through the window, espied the poor lady
sitting a little on one side in her arm-
chair, and her handkerchief had dropped on
the floor by her side; so what does the
little maid do but runs and fetches her mother
and some of the neighbours; and so they
raise the window and go in, and, sure
enough, they find the poor lady quite dead,
and as if she had been so for some days;
and she was nothing but skin and bone when
they took off her clothes. It is my opinion

she fretted herself to death after her companion; and so they have taken the poor lady—yesterday it was a week—and have laid her beside the other one in the churchyard, and there is ne'er a line to show who she was, any more than the other one. Even Lawyer Pearce, from Wadebridge, who came over here after the funeral, says he doesn't know who either of them was. But them lawyers don't always tell what they know, and it is my opinion he *must* know; for he went off to London in a great hurry after the first lady died, and had only but just come back on the day that the last funeral was."

"And is any one at the cottage now?" asked Trelawney in an agitated voice.

"Indeed, then, there is not, sir,—nor likely to be. For immediately after the funeral, Lawyer Pearce went up to the cottage along with Captain Will, and had every stitch of clothes and mortal thing

collected together that belonged to the
ladies. Sure they might have give some
of the clothes to the poor charwoman who
waited on them! But they didn't, and the
things were all huddled together, books and
all, and packed up in great boxes, and sent
off to London, as I have heard tell. And
the furniture has been all removed, and so
the house is as empty now as on the day
it was built."

To this account of the landlady's, little
remains to be added. From Lawyer Pearce,
whom he visited on his way through Wadebridge, Trelawney learnt that, acting under
instructions received from Sir Edward Arundel's nephew—a sister's son, who had succeeded to his property, though not to the
title—Mr. Wenlock had directed that the
secret of Lady Arundel's name and that
of her companion should be maintained,
and that, for the sake of avoiding scandal,

and sparing the feelings of Mr. Bertram, no publicity should be given to the circumstances under which Lady Arundel had died; no entry of her name or that of her companion was to be made in the parish register, or engraven on a stone. Accordingly no monument was ever erected to the memory of these unfortunate ladies, and the secret was so well kept by the few who were acquainted with the circumstances, that the names of the two recluses of St. Knighton's never transpired in the village, and has remained a mystery there down to the present hour.

As for the cottage, its ruined walls may still be seen, overgrown with weeds and brambles. For some time after the deaths of the ladies, a persevering effort was made by Captain Will to let the cottage. It figured for a long time amongst the advertisements in the county paper, under the

head of "To let," as "a, cottage most
romantically situated in a picturesque valley,
near a favourite waterfall, within a short
walk of the far-famed castle of TINTAGEL,
the birthplace of KING ARTHUR," "well
adapted for a summer residence," &c. &c.
But all would not do. The public manifested a decided repugnance to having anything to do with the cottage, or with a residence in the "haunted valley," as it began.
to be called. And, finally, Captain Will
was obliged to give up as hopeless the
idea of getting a tenant for his cottage; so
after disroofing the house and removing
the doors and windows and as much of
the woodwork as could be got at, he aban-
doned the place for the remainder of his
lease; and so it has been allowed to fall
into its present forlorn and ruinous condition.

As for Trelawney's after history, it may be

summed up in a few words. When the first shock was over, he felt more and more the necessity of active employment, if 'he was ever to regain peace of mind, or be aught else than a cumberer of the earth. Taking counsel, then, of the rector of St. Faith's— the church with the tapering spire pointing towards heaven, on which he had gazed when standing that summer morning on the top of Montacute Hill — Trelawney threw himself, heart and soul, into the work of his extensive parish; content with small results at first, but which brightened and became more hopeful every year, he gradually formed a nucleus of church feeling about him, and drew together a congregation; not large, indeed, but such as enabled him to celebrate the holy seasons of the Church in the Church's way, and to present a picture of a "reasonable, holy, and lively" service.

With active employment, health of mind
and health of body returned, and twelve
months had scarcely rolled over his head
before he stood the accepted suitor of
Charlotte Tressilian.

The family living might have been his
upon the death of his father, but Trelawney
had chosen his portion, and elected in preference to live and die amongst the Cornish
miners.

Mr. Bertram lived to an advanced age,
and to the last fostered the delusion that
his daughter, with her companion, had by
preference resided somewhere in the south of
England; he perseveringly ignored all that
related to the tragedy of St. Knighton's
Keive.

POSTSCRIPTUM.

In order to throw light upon some of the provincialisms which occur in the course of the story, as well as to amuse the reader, a few of the phrases and expressions which are in commonest use amongst the Cornish peasantry, are here set down in the shape of a glossary. They are given mostly from memory, with an occasional suggestion from a certain person at the writer's elbow. But, for some of the most expressive, and especially the foreignly-derived words, the writer is indebted to a talented Cornish

lady, whose attachment to her own native
soil, and interest in its old-world phrases
and customs, are only equalled by her
kindly home sympathies, which years have
not been able to chill, or intercourse with
the world to estrange.

GLOSSARY.

——◆◆◆——

Player, pleasure, " a fine deal of player."

Juice, use.

Passivanting, pursuing a headlong course (*i. e.* dashing along);
  derived, probably, from the French *poursuivre,* or *poursuivant.*

Planching, flooring.

Corracy, an old grudge, derived, perhaps, from the French
  corrasif du cœur.

Vent, to sell (from *vendre*).

Scabble-and-gow, tumultuous talking, as amongst angry women.

Mingle-cum-por, a medley.

Stir a couse, bustling.

Capper-house, noise, stir.

Thirl, empty, hollow.

Leary, nearly the same signification.

Clunk, to swallow.

Stank, to trample.

Fouche, to push.   To *fouch-along* is nearly synonymous with the
  phrase of " making both ends meet," or, " keeping the head
  above water."

Ballyrag, to vituperate.   (*Qu.* Imported from the sister isle ?)

A swogger, a scolding.

Randigale, a concourse of people.

Padgetty-pows, lizards.

Jaleing, labouring strenuously.

Jaleing-along, laborious walking.

Trapesing, a lazy, loitering course.

Scat, a heap, plenty, as " a scat of fine weather."

Murely, truly, literally.

Fouse, to rumple.

Fang, to realize, to make sure of.

Likely, comely.

Slock-away, to take slyly.

Soase, a friendly interjection, analogous to gossip.

Leuth, a sheltered place.

Quilquin, a frog.

Leu, sheltered.

Coosing, gossipping.

Uprised, " churched."

Upscud, spilt, upset.

Figgy, made of raisins, e. g., a plum-pudding.

Squab-pie, a pie composed of mutton, onions, apples, raisins, sugar, salt, and spice—a great favourite with the Cornish.

Feast'n Sunday, answering to our Wake Sunday.

" *A good churchman* " means a clergyman possessed of strong voice (not " views ")—one who can " make himself heard."

Brave, considerable, as a " *brave bit*," a " good step," as we should say.

A " *bra' keenly mine*," a mine likely to do well.

Tender-dear, a term of endearment applied to children.

Spell of work, a piece of work.

Grass-captain, a subordinate mine " captain " employed above the surface, in contradistinction to an *underground captain*, employed under the surface.

Day-corps—night-corps, the gang of miners who work by day, and night, respectively. The day and night work alternates weekly, or, in some cases, fortnightly. A *spell* of work is for eight hours.

Adventurers, those who work the mine. " *Simple* " ditto, those who bear the loss.

" *The lord*," the proprietor of the land where a mine is sunk.

A "*dish*," the "lord's" share, an eighteenth of the ore raised.

Fitty, neat, suitable.

Benefits of a living, the tithes, and income generally.

Barton, farm-yard.

Church-town, any collection of houses about a church.

Town-place, the buildings in a farm-yard.

Drisky, misty, foggy. "A Cornishman is never in such spirits as in drisky weather."

Un', for uncle, applied to seniors indifferently, as *An'*, for aunt, applied in the same way.

Every young man is "*my son*," as every young girl is "*my little maid*."

Shape, a mess, disorder.

To carney, to wheedle, to coax.

Cheal-vean, a little child.

Cairn, a pile of rock.

Porth, a cove.

Play-gay, a plaything.

Star-a-gaze pie, a mackerel pie with the heads above the paste, gazing upwards, as it were.

Palched, weak, sickly, as a "palched man."

Bal, the surface of a mine, as "going to bal."

Kidleywink, a public-house.

Spirty, spirited, as a "spirty cheal."

Shrim, a creeping cold.

Fouthiest, forwardest.

Crum, a bit.

To marrinade, is to pickle, as "marrinaded fish."

For the noanes, for the nonce, or occasion.

All a samsawdled and jabbled up, i.e., bad cooking.

A blast of fuzz, i.e., a faggot of furze.

Furmades or Fairmaids. (*Qu.* Fumades?) Pilchards.

A pitch, a piece of work.

Curls, carols.

Gnarly, cross-grained.

" *Brave,*" " *clever,*" " *charming,*" in good health, that is.

Tre, a *town, i.e.,* a house and buildings ; *Pol,* a piece of water ;
 Pen, a head, or headland.

Some of the Cornish *names,* too, are very peculiar. Thus of
" Christian" names, Hanibal, Zenobia, Boadicea, Lavinia, and
Lucretia, are all favourites, and amongst surnames, we find—
Penaluna, Pallamountain, Pucky, Botheras, Jacka, Polkinghorne, &c. But, generally speaking, especially in the mining
districts, these are plainly borrowed from Christian names ; thus
almost every miner answers to the name of Richards, Harry,
Johns, James, Rogers, Thomas, Edwards, or some such names—
a Christian name obviously turned into a surname.

THE END.

London : Smith, Elder and Co., Little Green Arbour Court, Old Bailey, E.C.